"I—I don't know how you can pretend like this," Helen said haltingly.

Marc's faint smile was crooked. "But I am not pretending, *chérie,*" he told her quietly. "I want you. I have made no secret of it."

She stared down at the tablecloth. "Then you're due for a serious disappointment, Monsieur Delaroche. Even if I was in the market for an affair—which I'm not—you'd be the last person on earth I'd choose."

"Then at least we agree on something," Marc drawled. "Because I do not want an affair either. *Au contraire,* I wish you to become my wife...."

SARA CRAVEN was born in south Devon, England, and grew up surrounded by books in a house by the sea. After leaving school she worked as a local journalist, covering everything from flower shows to murders, before embarking on a long and successful career writing for Harlequin Presents®. Apart from writing, Sara's passions include films, music, cooking and eating in good restaurants. She now lives in the county of Somerset, England.

IN THE MILLIONAIRE'S POSSESSION

SARA CRAVEN

THE MILLIONAIRE AFFAIR

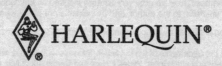

HARLEQUIN®

TORONTO • NEW YORK • LONDON
AMSTERDAM • PARIS • SYDNEY • HAMBURG
STOCKHOLM • ATHENS • TOKYO • MILAN • MADRID
PRAGUE • WARSAW • BUDAPEST • AUCKLAND

ISBN 0-373-82026-7

IN THE MILLIONAIRE'S POSSESSION

First North American Publication 2005.

www.eHarlequin.com

Printed in U.S.A.

CHAPTER ONE

HELEN had never been so nervous in her life.

The starkness of her surroundings did not help, of course.

This was, after all, the London headquarters of Restauration International—an organisation supposedly devoted to historical conservation projects.

She'd expected panelled walls hung with works of art, antique furniture, and possibly a Persian carpet. Something with the grace and charm of the past.

Instead she'd been greeted by a receptionist with attitude, and dumped in this glass and chrome box with only a water cooler for company as the long, slow nerve-racking minutes passed.

And although she had to admit that the arrangement of canvas slats that formed her chair was surprisingly comfortable, it couldn't make her feel at ease mentally.

But then, in this life or death situation, what could?

Her hands tightened on the handle of her briefcase as she ran a silent check on the points she needed to make once she came face to face with the directors of Restauration International.

They're my last hope now, she thought. Every other source has dried up. So I need to get it right.

Suddenly restless, she walked across to the cooler and filled a paper cup. As she moved, she saw the security camera become activated, and repressed a grimace at the idea that unseen eyes at some control point might be watching her.

'Look businesslike,' her friend Lottie had advised her. 'Get out of those eternal jeans and put on a skirt. Remember you're making a presentation, not mucking out the ruins. You've had a lot of help over this,' she added with mock sternness. 'So don't blow it.'

And Lottie was quite right, Helen thought soberly. So many people had rallied round with quite amazing kindness. Checking the draft of her written report and making suggestions. Providing quick facelifts to the outside buildings and grounds with painting and weeding parties, in case the committee came to see the place for themselves. And even offering films of various events held at Monteagle over the past couple of years to use in the video, itself the result of a favour that had been called in by Lottie.

But now, at last, it was all down to her. She'd taken her friend's advice and put on her one good grey skirt, teaming it with a demure white cotton blouse and her elderly black blazer. Hopefully they wouldn't look too closely and see the shabbiness of her attire, she thought.

Her light brown hair—which badly needed cutting and shaping, when she had the time and the money—had been drawn back severely from her face and confined at the nape of her neck by a black ribbon bow, and there were small silver studs in the lobes of her ears.

Not much there for the hidden spectator to criticise, she thought, resisting the impulse to raise her cup in salute.

She made the trip back to her chair look deliberately casual, as if she didn't have a care in the world and there was nothing much riding on the coming interview.

Only my entire life, she thought, as her taut throat accepted the cool water. Only everything I care most about in the world now at the mercy of strangers.

Apart from Nigel, of course, she amended hastily.

Somehow I have to convince them that Monteagle is worth saving. That I'm not going to give up the struggle like my father and Grandpa and watch the place slide into total oblivion. Or, worse still, into the hands of Trevor Newson.

She shuddered at the memory of the fleshy, complacent face awaiting with a smile the victory that he thought was inevitable. Counting the days until he could turn Monteagle into the gross medieval theme park he'd set his heart on.

It had been those plans, as outlined to her, that had sent her on this last desperate quest to find the money for the house's urgently needed repairs.

All the other organisations that she'd doggedly approached had rejected her pleas for a grant on the grounds that Monteagle was too small, too unimportant, and too far off the normal tourist trails.

'Which is why it needs me,' Trevor Newson had told her. 'Jousting on the lawns, pig roasts, banqueting in the great hall…' His eyes glistened. 'That'll put it on the map, all right. The coach parties will flock here, and so will foreign tourists once I get it on the internet. And don't keep me waiting too long for your answer,' he added. 'Or the price I'm offering will start to go down.'

'You need not wait at all,' Helen said with icy civility. 'The answer is no, Mr Newson.'

'And now you're being hasty,' he chided in the patronising tone she so resented. 'After all, what choice have you got? The place is falling down around you, and it's common knowledge your father and grandfather left little but debts when they died.'

He ticked off on his fingers. 'You've got the rent from the grazing land and a bit of income from the handful of visitors who come when you open the place up each summer, and that won't get you far. In fact, it's a wonder you've hung on as long as you have.'

He gave a pitying shake of the head. 'You need to sell, my dear. And if you really can't bear to leave and move away I might even be able to offer you some work. These tournaments used to have a Queen of Love and Beauty presiding over them, apparently, and you're a good-looking girl.' He leered at her. 'I can just see you, properly made-up, in some low-cut medieval dress.'

'It's a tempting offer,' Helen said, controlling her temper by a whisker. 'But I'm afraid the answer's still no.'

'Ghastly old lech,' Lottie had commented. 'Better not tell Nigel, or he might deck him.' She'd paused. 'Is he going with you to confront this committee?'

'No.' Helen had resolutely concealed her disappointment.

'He's incredibly busy at work right now. Anyway,' she'd
added, 'I'm a grown up girl. I can cope.'

As Nigel himself had said, she recalled with a pang. And
maybe she'd simply taken too much for granted in counting on
his support today. But they'd been seeing each other for a long
time now, and everyone in the area presumed that he'd be
fighting at her side in the battle to save Monteagle.

In fact, as Helen admitted to no one but herself, Nigel had
been pretty lukewarm about her struggles to retain her home.
He wasn't a poor man by any means—he worked in a merchant
bank, and had inherited money from his grandmother as well—
but he'd never offered any practical form of help.

It was something they would really need to discuss—once
she got the grant. Because she was determined to be self-
sufficient, and, while she drew the line at Mr Newson's theme
park, she had several other schemes in mind to boost the
house's earning power.

Although lately they hadn't had the opportunity to talk about
very much at all, she realised with a faint frown. But that was
probably her fault in the main. Nigel's work had kept him
confined to London recently, but she'd been so totally en-
grossed in preparing her case for the committee that she'd
barely missed him.

What a thing to admit about the man you were going to
marry!

But all that was going to change, she vowed remorsefully.
Once today was over, win or lose, it was going to be permanent
commitment from now on. Everything he'd ever asked from
her. Including *that*.

She knew she was probably being an old-fashioned idiot,
and most of her contemporaries would laugh if they knew, but
she'd always veered away from the idea of sex before marriage.

Not that she was scared of surrender, she thought defensively, or unsure of her own feelings for Nigel. It was just that
when she stood with him in the village church to make her
vows she wanted him to know that she was his alone, and that
her white dress meant something.

On a more practical level, it had never seemed to be quite the right moment, either.

Never the time, the place, and the loved one altogether, she thought, grimacing inwardly. But she couldn't expect Nigel to be patient for ever, not when they belonged together. So why hold back any longer?

She was startled out of her reverie by the sudden opening of the door. Helen got hurriedly to her feet, to be confronted by a blonde girl, tall and slim, with endless legs, and wearing a smart black suit. She gave Helen a swift formal smile while her eyes swept her with faint disparagement.

'Miss Frayne? Will you come with me, please? The committee is waiting for you.'

'And I've been waiting for the committee,' Helen told her coolly.

She was led down a long narrow corridor, with walls plastered in a Greek key pattern. It made her feel slightly giddy, and she wondered if this was a deliberate ploy.

Her companion flung open the door at the far end. 'Miss Frayne,' she announced, and stood back to allow Helen to precede her into the room.

More concrete, thought Helen, taking a swift look around. More metal, more glass. And seven men standing at an oblong table, acknowledging her presence with polite inclinations of their heads.

'Please, Miss Frayne, sit. Be comfortable.' The speaker, clearly the chairman, was opposite her. He was a bearded man with grey hair and glasses, who looked Scandinavian.

Helen sank down on to a high-backed affair of leather and steel, clutching her briefcase on her lap while they all took their places.

They looked like clones of each other, she thought, in their neat dark suits and discreetly patterned ties, sitting bolt upright round the table. Except for one, she realised. The man casually lounging in the seat to the right of the chairman.

He was younger than his colleagues—early to mid-thirties, Helen judged—with an untidy mane of black hair and a swarthy face that no one would ever describe as handsome. He had a beak of a nose, and a thin-lipped, insolent mouth, while eyes, dark and impenetrable as the night, studied her from under heavy lids.

Unlike the rest of the buttoned-up committee members, he looked as if he'd just crawled out of bed and thrown on the clothing that was nearest to hand. Moreover, his tie had been pulled loose and the top of his shirt left undone.

He had the appearance of someone who'd strayed in off the street by mistake, she thought critically.

And saw his mouth twist into a faint grin, as if he'd divined what she was thinking and found it amusing.

Helen felt a kind of embarrassed resentment at being so transparent. This was not how she'd planned to begin at all. She gave him a cold look, and saw his smile widen in sensuous, delighted appreciation.

Making her realise, for the first time in her life, that a man did not have to be conventionally handsome to blaze charm and a lethal brand of sexual attraction.

Helen felt as if she'd been suddenly subjected to a force field of male charisma, and she resented it. And the fact that he had beautiful teeth did nothing to endear him to her either.

'Be comfortable,' the chairman had said.

My God, she thought. What a hope. Because she'd never felt more awkward in her life. Or so scared.

She took a deep breath and transferred her attention deliberately to the chairman, trying to concentrate as he congratulated her on the depth and lucidity of her original application for a grant, and on the additional material she'd supplied to back up her claim.

They all had their folders open, she saw, except one. And no prizes for guessing which of them it was, she thought indignantly. But at least she wasn't the object of his attention any longer. Instead, her swift sideways glance told her, he seemed to be staring abstractedly into space, as if he was miles away.

If only, thought Helen, steadying her flurried breathing. And, anyway, why serve on the committee if he wasn't prepared to contribute to its work?

He didn't even react when she produced the videotape. 'I hope this will give you some idea of the use Monteagle has been put to in the recent past,' she said. 'I intend to widen the scope of activities in future—even have the house licensed for weddings.'

There were murmurs of polite interest and approval, and she began to relax a little—only to realise that he was staring at her once again, his eyes travelling slowly over her face and down, she realised furiously, to the swell of her breasts against the thin blouse. She tried to behave as if she was unconscious of his scrutiny, but felt the betrayal of warm blood invading her face. Finally, to her relief, the dark gaze descended to her small bare hands, clasped tensely on the table in front of her.

'You plan to marry there yourself, perhaps, *mademoiselle*?' He had a low, resonant voice which was not unattractive, she admitted unwillingly, still smarting from the overt sensuality of his regard. And his English was excellent, in spite of his French accent.

She wondered how he'd taken the section of her report which stated that the fortified part of Monteagle had been built at the time of the Hundred Years War, and that the Black Prince, France's most feared enemy, had often stayed there.

Now she lifted her chin and met his enquiring gaze with a flash of her long-lashed hazel eyes, wishing at the same time that she and Nigel were officially engaged and she had a ring to wear.

'Yes,' she said. 'As a matter of fact, I do, *monsieur*. I thought I might even be the first one,' she added with a flash of inspiration.

Of course she hadn't discussed this with Nigel, she reminded herself guiltily, but she didn't see what objection he could have. And it would make the most wonderful setting—besides providing useful publicity at the same time.

'But how romantic,' he murmured, and relapsed into his reverie again.

After that questions from the other committee members came thick and fast, asking her to explain or expand further on some of the points she'd made in her application. Clearly they'd all read the file, she thought hopefully, and seemed genuinely interested in what she had to say.

The door opened to admit the tall blonde, bringing coffee on a trolley, and Helen was glad to see there was mineral water as well. This interview was proving just as much of an ordeal as she'd expected, and her mouth was dry again.

When the blonde withdrew, the Frenchman reached for his folder and extracted a sheet of paper.

'This is not your first application for financial assistance towards the repair and renovation of Monteagle House, *mademoiselle*. Is this an accurate list of the organisations you have previously approached?'

Helen bit her lip as she scanned down the column of names. 'Yes, it is.'

'But none of your efforts were successful?' The low voice pressed her.

'No,' she admitted stonily, aware that her creamy skin had warmed.

'So how did you become aware of us?'

'A friend of mine found you on the internet. She said you seemed to be interested in smaller projects. So—I thought I would try.'

'Because you were becoming desperate.' It was a statement, not a question.

'Yes.' Helen looked at him defiantly. Her consciousness of her surroundings seemed to have contracted—intensified. There might just have been the two of them in the room, locked in confrontation. 'By this stage I will explore any avenue that presents itself. I will not allow Monteagle to become derelict, and I'll do whatever it takes to save it.'

There was a silence, then he produced another sheet of paper. 'The surveyor's report that you have included in your submission is twenty years old.'

'Yes,' she said. 'I felt that the recommendations made then still apply. Although the costs have obviously risen.'

'Twenty years is a long time, *mademoiselle*. Having commissioned such a report, why did your family not carry out the necessary works at that time?'

Helen's flush deepened. 'My grandfather had every intention of doing so, but he was overtaken by events.'

'Can you explain further?' the smooth voice probed.

She took a breath, hating the admission she was being forced to make. 'There was a crisis in the insurance industry. My grandfather was a Lloyds' name in those days, and the calls that were made on him brought us all to the edge of ruin. He even thought Monteagle might have to be sold.'

'That is still a possibility, of course,' her adversary said gently, and paused. 'Is it not true that you have received a most generous offer for the entire estate from a Monsieur Trevor Newson? An offer that would halt the disintegration of the house, *mademoiselle*, and in addition restore your own finances? Would that not be better than having to beg your way round every committee and trust? And deal with constant rejection?'

'I find Mr Newson's plans for the estate totally unacceptable,' Helen said curtly. 'I'm a Frayne, and I won't allow the place that has been our home for centuries to be trashed in the way he proposes. I refuse to give up.' She leaned forward, her voice shaking with sudden intensity. 'I'll find the money somehow, and I'll do anything to get it.'

'Anything?' The dark brows lifted mockingly. 'You are a most determined champion of your cause.'

'I have to be.' Helen flung back her head. 'And if achieving my aim includes begging, then so be it. Monteagle is well worth the sacrifice.'

And then, as if a wire had snapped, parting them, it was over. The Frenchman was leaning back in his chair and the chairman was rising to his feet.

'It has been a pleasure to meet you, Miss Frayne, and we shall consider your proposals with great care—including the additional information and material you have supplied.' He picked up the video, giving her a warm smile. 'We hope to come to our decision by the end of the month.'

'I'm grateful to you for seeing me,' Helen said formally, and got herself out of the room without once glancing in the direction of her interrogator.

In the corridor, she paused, a hand pressed to her side as if she had been running in some uphill race.

What in hell had been going on there? she asked herself dazedly. Were they running some good cop/bad cop routine, where the upright members of the committee softened her up with their kindly interest so that their resident thug could move in for the kill?

Up to then it had been going quite well, she thought anxiously, or she'd believed it had. But her audience might not appreciate being regarded as the very last resort at the end of a long list of them, as he'd suggested.

God, but he'd been loathsome in every respect, she thought vengefully as she made her way back to the reception area. And to hell with his charm and sex appeal.

Quite apart from anything else, she knew now what it was like to be mentally undressed, and it was a technique that she did not appreciate. In fact, she thought furiously, it was probably a form of sexual harassment—not that anyone whose spiritual home was obviously the Stone Age would have heard of such a thing, or even care.

All the same, she found herself wondering who he was exactly and how much influence he actually wielded in Restauration International. Well, there was one quick way to find out.

The blonde was in the foyer, chatting to the receptionist. They both glanced up with brief formal smiles as Helen approached.

She said coolly, 'Please may I have a copy of the organisation's introduction pack?'

Brows rose, and they exchanged glances. The blonde said, 'I think you'll find you were sent one following your original enquiry, Miss Frayne.'

'Indeed I was,' Helen agreed. 'But unfortunately it's at home, and there are a few details I need to check.' She paused. 'So—if it's not too much trouble...?'

There was another exchange of glances, then the receptionist opened with ill grace a drawer in her large desk, and took out a plastic-encased folder, which she handed to Helen.

'One per application is the norm, Miss Frayne,' she said. 'Please look after it.'

'I shall treasure it,' Helen assured her. As she moved to put the pack in her briefcase, she was suddenly aware of footsteps crossing the foyer behind her. And at the same time, as if some switch had been pulled, the haughty stares from the other two girls vanished, to be replaced by smiles so sweet that they were almost simpering.

Helen felt as if icy fingers were tracing a path down her spine as instinct told her who had come to join them.

She turned slowly to face him, schooling her expression to indifference.

'Making sure I leave the building, *monsieur*?'

'No, merely going to my own next appointment, *mademoiselle*.' His smile mocked her quite openly. He glanced at the pack she was still holding. 'And my name is Delaroche,' he added softly. 'Marc Delaroche. As I would have told you earlier, had you asked.'

He watched with undisguised appreciation as Helen struggled against an urge to hurl the pack at his head, then made her a slight bow as upbringing triumphed over instinct and she replaced it on the desk.

She said icily, 'I merely wanted something to read on the train. But I can always buy a paper.'

'But of course.' He was using that smile again, but this time she was braced against its impact.

'*A bientôt,*' he added, and went, with a wave to the other two, who were still gazing at him in a kind of dumb entrancement.

'See you soon', Monsieur Delaroche? Helen asked silently after his retreating back. Is that what you just said to me? She drew a deep breath. My God, not if I see you first.

She was disturbingly aware of that same brief shiver of ice along her nerve-endings. As if in some strange way she was being warned.

* * *

Marc Delaroche had said he had an appointment, but all the same Helen was thankful to find him nowhere in sight when she got outside the building.

She'd thought her nervousness would dissipate now that the interview was over, but she was wrong. She felt lost, somehow, and ridiculously scared. Perhaps it was just the noise and dirt of London that was upsetting her, she thought, wondering how Nigel could relish working here amid all this uproar.

But at least she could seize the opportunity of seeing him while she was here, she told herself, producing her mobile phone. Before she got her train back to the peace of the countryside and Monteagle.

He answered at once, but he was clearly not alone because she could hear voices and laughter in the background, and the clink of glasses.

'Helen?' He sounded astonished. 'Where are you ringing from?'

'Groverton Street,' she said. 'It isn't too far from where you work.' She paused. 'I thought maybe you'd buy me lunch.'

'Lunch?' he echoed. 'I don't think I can. I'm a bit tied up. You should have told me in advance you were coming up today, and I'd have made sure I was free.'

'But I did tell you,' Helen said, trying to stifle her disappointment. 'I've just had my interview with Restauration International—remember?'

'Oh, God,' he said. 'Yes, of course. I've been so busy it completely slipped my mind.' He paused. 'How did it go anyway?'

'Pretty well, I think—I hope.' Helen tried to dismiss the thought of Marc Delaroche from her mind.

One man, she thought. One dissenting voice. What harm could he really do?

'They seemed interested,' she added. 'Sympathetic—for the most part. And they said I'd know by the end of the month, so I've less than ten days to wait.'

'Well, I'll keep my fingers crossed for you,' Nigel said. 'And maybe—under the circumstances—I could manage lunch after all. Celebrate a little. It's certainly the most hopeful result you've had.' He paused again. 'I'll need to pull a few strings, change things around a little, but it should be all right. Meet me at the Martinique at one clock.'

'But I don't know where it is,' she protested.

'But the cab driver will,' he said with a touch of exasperation. 'It's new, and pretty trendy. Everyone's going there.'

'Then will we get a table?' Helen asked, wondering, troubled, whether she could afford the price of a taxi.

He sighed. 'Helen, you're so naïve. The bank has a standing reservation there. It's not a problem. Now, I must go. See you later.'

She switched off her phone and replaced it slowly in her bag. It sounded rather as if Nigel had gone to this Martinique place already. But then why shouldn't he? she reminded herself impatiently. Entertaining the bank's clients at smart restaurants was part of his job. It was all part of the world he inhabited, along with platinum cards, endless taxis, and first-class tickets everywhere.

Yet she'd travelled up on a cheap day return, needed to count her pennies, and most of her entertaining involved cheese on toast or pasta, with a bottle of cheap plonk shared with Lottie or another girlfriend.

Nigel belonged to a different world, she thought with a pang, and it would require a quantum leap on her part to join him there.

But I can do it, she told herself, unfastening the constriction of the black ribbon bow and shaking her hair loose almost defiantly. I can do anything—even save Monteagle. And nothing's going to stop me.

Her moment of euphoria was brought to a halt by the realisation that lack of funds might well prevent her from completing even the minor mission of reaching the restaurant to meet Nigel.

However, with the help of her *A to Z* and a copy of *Time Out*, she discovered that the Martinique was just over a mile away. Easy walking distance, she decided, setting off at a brisk pace.

She found it without difficulty, although the search had left her hot and thirsty.

Its smart black and white awning extended over the pavement, shading terracotta pots of evergreens. Helen took a deep breath and walked in. She found herself in a small reception area, being given a questioning look by a young man behind a desk.

'*Mademoiselle* has a reservation?'

'Well, not exactly—' she began, and was interrupted by an immediate shake of the head.

'I regret that we are fully booked. Perhaps another day we can have the pleasure of serving *mademoiselle*.'

She said quickly, 'I'm joining someone—a Mr Nigel Hartley.'

He gave her a surprised look, then glanced at the large book in front of him. 'Yes, he has a table at one o clock, but he has not yet arrived.' He paused. 'Would you like to enjoy a drink at the bar? Or be seated to wait for him.'

'I'd like to sit down, please.'

'*D'accord.*' He came from behind the desk. 'May I take your jacket?' He indicated the blazer she was carrying over her arm.

'Oh—no. No, thank you,' Helen said, remembering with acute embarrassment that the lining was slightly torn.

'Then please follow me.' He opened a door, and what seemed like a wall of sound came to meet her, so that she almost flinched.

Nigel had not exaggerated the restaurant's popularity, she thought. She found herself in a large bright room, with windows on two sides and more tables crammed into the rest of it than she would have believed possible. Every table seemed to be occupied, and the noise was intense, but she squeezed through the sea of white linen, crystal and silver after her guide and discovered there were a few remaining inches of space in one corner.

She sank down thankfully on to one of the high-backed wooden chairs, wishing that it were possible to kick off her shoes.

'May I bring something for *mademoiselle*?' The young man hovered.

'Just some still water, please,' she returned.

She had no doubt that the Martinique was a trendy place—somewhere to see and be seen—but she wished Nigel had chosen something quieter. She also wished very much that it wasn't a French restaurant either. Too reminiscent, she thought, of her recent interrogation.

She wanted to talk to Nigel, but the kind of private conversation she had in mind could hardly be conducted at the tops of their voices.

He clearly thought she'd enjoy a taste of the high life, she decided ruefully, and she must be careful not to give him a hint of her disappointment at his choice.

Besides, they would have the rest of their lives to talk.

He was already ten minutes late, she realised, and was just beginning to feel self-conscious about sitting on her own when a waiter appeared with a bottle of mineral water and a tumbler containing ice cubes. The tray also held a tall slender glass filled with a rich pink liquid, fizzing gently.

'I'm afraid I didn't order this,' Helen protested, as he placed it in front of her. 'What is it?'

'Kir Royale, *mademoiselle*—champagne and *cassis*—and it comes with the compliments of *monsieur*.'

'Oh,' she said with relief. Nigel must have phoned through the order, she thought, as a peace offering for his tardiness. It was the kind of caring gesture she should have expected, and it made her feel better—happier about the situation as a whole.

She drank some water to refresh her mouth, then sipped the kir slowly, enjoying the faint fragrance of the blackcurrant and the sheer lift of the wine.

But she couldn't make it last for ever, and by the time she'd drained the glass Nigel still hadn't arrived. She was beginning to get nervous and irritated in equal measure.

She beckoned to the waiter. 'Has there been any further message from *monsieur* to say he's been delayed?' she asked. 'Because, if not, I'd like another kir.'

He looked bewildered. 'There is no delay, *mademoiselle*. *Monsieur* is here at this moment, having lunch. Shall I consult him on your behalf?'

Helen stared at him. 'He's *here*? You must be mistaken.'

'No, *mademoiselle*. See—there by the window.'

Helen looked, and what she saw made her throat close in shock. It was Marc Delaroche, she realised numbly, seated at a table with two other men. He was listening to what they were saying, but, as if he instantly sensed Helen focussing on him, he glanced round and met her horrified gaze. He inclined his head in acknowledgement, then reached for his own glass, lifting it in a swift and silent toast.

She disengaged from him instantly, flushed and mortified. She said, 'You mean he—that person—sent me this drink?' She took a deep breath, forcing herself back to a semblance of composure, even though her heart was racing unevenly. 'I—I didn't know that. And I certainly wouldn't dream of having another. In fact, perhaps you'd bring me the bill for this one, plus the water, and I'll just—leave.'

'But you have not yet had lunch,' the waiter protested. 'And besides, here comes Monsieur Hartley.'

And sure enough it was Nigel, striding across the restaurant as if conducting a personal parting of the Red Sea, tall, blond and immaculate, in his dark blue pinstripe and exquisitely knotted silk tie.

'So there you are,' he greeted her.

'It's where I've been for the past half hour,' Helen told him evenly. 'What happened?'

'Well, I warned you I was busy.' He dropped a cursory kiss on her cheek as he passed. 'Menus, please, Gaspard. I'm pushed for time today. In fact, I won't bother with the *carte*. I'll just have steak, medium rare, with a mixed salad.'

'Then I'll have the same,' Helen said. 'I wouldn't want to keep you waiting.'

'Fine.' He either ignored or didn't notice the irony in her tone. 'And a bottle of house red, Gaspard. Quick as you can. Plus a gin and tonic.' He glanced at Helen. 'Do you want a drink, sweetie?'

'I've already had one,' she said. 'Kir Royale, as a matter of fact.'

His lips thinned a little. 'Rather a new departure for you, isn't it? Did the waiter talk you into it?'

'No,' she said. 'But don't worry. One is more than enough.'
She was ashamed to hear how acerbic she sounded, and it was
all the fault of that—that *creature* across the room. But she
was sharing precious time with the man she loved, and she
wouldn't allow it to be spoiled by anyone or anything.

She made herself smile at Nigel, and put her hand on his.
'It's so great to see you,' she said gently. 'Do you realise how
long it's been?'

He sighed. 'I know, but life at work is so hectic just now I
hardly have any time to spare.'

'Your parents must miss you too.'

He shrugged. 'They're far too busy planning Dad's retirement and giving the house a pre-sale facelift to worry about
me.' He shot her a swift glance. 'You did know they're moving
to Portugal in the near future?'

'Selling Oaktree House?' Helen said slowly. 'I had no idea.'
She gave him a blank look. 'But how will you manage? It's
your home.'

'Off and on for the past ten years, yes,' Nigel said with a
touch of impatience. 'But my life's in London now. I'm going
to stop renting and look for somewhere to buy. Ah, my drink
at last. My God, I could do with it. I've had a hell of a morning.' And he launched himself into a description of its vicis-
situdes which was still going strong when their food arrived.

Not that Helen was particularly hungry. Her appetite, such
as it was, seemed to have suddenly dissipated. Nor was she
giving her full attention to the vagaries of the financial markets
and the irresponsible attitude of certain nameless clients, as
outlined by Nigel. Her mind was on another track altogether.

Something had happened, she thought numbly. Some fun-
damental shift had taken place and she hadn't noticed.

Well, she was totally focussed now, because this involved
her life too. She'd assumed that Nigel would live with her at
Monteagle once they were married, and commute to London.
After all, she couldn't move away, use Monteagle as a weekend
home. Surely he realised that.

But there was no way they could talk about it now. Not with

Nigel glancing at his watch every couple of minutes as he rapidly forked up his steak.

Eventually she broke into his monologue. 'Nigel—this weekend, we have to talk. Can you come over—spend the day with me on Sunday?'

'Not this weekend, I'm afraid. It's the chairman's birthday, and he's celebrating with a weekend party at his place in Sussex, so duty calls.' His smile was swift and light. 'And now I have to dash. I have a two-thirty meeting. The bill goes straight to my office, so order yourself a pudding if you want, darling, and coffee. See you later.' He blew her a kiss, and was gone.

Once again she was sitting alone, she thought as she pushed her plate away. A fact that would doubtless not be lost on her adversary across the room. She risked a lightning glance from under her lashes, and realised with a surge of relief that his table was empty and being cleared. At least he hadn't witnessed her cavalier treatment at Nigel's hands. Nor would she have to grit her teeth and thank him for that bloody drink. With luck, she would never have to set eyes on him again. End of story.

She'd wanted this to be a great day in her life, she thought with a silent sigh, but since she'd first set eyes on Marc Delaroche it seemed to have been downhill all the way.

And now she had better go and catch her train. She was just reaching for her bag when Gaspard arrived, bearing a tray which he placed in front of her with a flourish.

'There must be some mistake,' Helen protested, watching him unload a cafetière, cups, saucers, two glasses and a bottle of armagnac. 'I didn't order any of this.'

'But I did,' Marc Delaroche said softly. 'Because you look as if you need it. So do not refuse me, *ma belle, je vous en prie*.'

And before she could utter any kind of protest, he took the seat opposite her, so recently vacated by Nigel, and smiled into her startled eyes.

CHAPTER TWO

'I THOUGHT you'd gone.' The words were out before she could stop herself, implying that she took even a remote interest in his actions.

'I was merely bidding *au revoir* to my friends.' He filled her cup from the cafetière. 'Before returning to offer you a *digestif*.' He poured a judicious amount of armagnac into each crystal bowl, and pushed one towards her. 'Something your companion should consider, perhaps,' he added meditatively. 'If he continues to rush through his meals at such a rate he will have an ulcer before he is forty.'

'Thank you.' Helen lifted her chin. 'I'll be sure to pass your warning on to him.'

'I intended it for you,' he said. 'I presume he is the man you plan to marry at Monteagle with such panache?' He slanted a smile at her. 'After all, it is a wife's duty to look after the physical well-being of her husband—in every way. Don't you think so?'

'You don't want to know what I think.' Helen bit her lip. 'You really are some kind of dinosaur.'

His smile widened. 'And a man with a ruined digestion is an even more savage beast, believe me,' he told her softly. 'Just as a beautiful girl left alone in a restaurant is an offence against nature.' He raised his glass. *Salut.'*

'Oh, spare me.' Helen gritted her teeth. 'I don't need your compliments—or your company.'

'Perhaps not,' he said. 'But you require my vote on the committee, so maybe you should force yourself to be civil for this short time, and drink with me.'

Smouldering, Helen drank some of her coffee. 'What made you choose this restaurant particularly?' she asked, after a loaded pause.

His brows lifted mockingly. 'You suspect some sinister motive? That I am following you, perhaps?' He shook his head. 'You are wrong. I was invited here by my companions—who have a financial interest in the place and wished my opinion. Also I arrived first, remember, so I could accuse you of stalking me.'

Helen stiffened. 'That, of course, is just *so* likely.' Her tone bit.

'No,' he returned coolly. 'To my infinite regret, it is not likely at all.'

Helen felt her throat muscles tighten warily. 'Why are you doing this? Buying me drinks—forcing your company on me?'

He shrugged. 'Because I wished to encounter you when you were more relaxed. When you had—let your hair down, as they say.' He leaned back in his chair. 'It looks much better loose, so why scrape it back in that unbecoming way?'

'I wanted to look businesslike for the interview,' she returned coldly. 'Not as if I was trading on my gender.'

'Put like that,' he said, 'I find it unappealing too.'

'So why are you ignoring my obvious wish to keep my distance?'

He lifted his glass, studying the colour of the armagnac. He said, 'Your fiancé arrived late and left early. Perhaps I am merely trying to compensate for his lack of attention.'

She bit her lip. 'How dare you criticise him? You know nothing at all about him. He happens to be working very hard for our future together—and I don't feel neglected in any way,' she added defiantly.

'I am relieved to hear it, *ma mie*,' he drawled. 'I feared for your sake that his performance in bed might be conducted at the same speed as your lunch dates.'

She stared at him, shocked into a sudden blush that reached the roots of her hair.

Her voice shook. 'You have no right to talk to me like that— to speculate about my private relationships in that—disgusting way. You should be ashamed of yourself.'

He looked back at her without a glimmer of repentance. 'It was prompted solely by my concern for your happiness, I assure you.'

She pushed back her chair and got to her feet, fumbling for her jacket. She said jerkily, 'When I get the money to restore Monteagle I shall fill the world with my joy, *monsieur*. And that is the only affair of mine in which you have the right to probe. Goodbye.'

She walked past him and out of the restaurant, her face still burning but her head held proudly.

It was only when she was outside, heading for the tube station, that she realised just how afraid she'd been that he would follow her—stop her from leaving in some unspecified way.

But of course he had not done so.

He's just a predator, she thought, looking for potential prey and testing their weaknesses. He saw I was alone, and possibly vulnerable, so he moved in. That's all that happened.

Or was it?

If only I hadn't blushed, she castigated herself. I just hope he interprets it as anger, not embarrassment.

Because she couldn't bear him to know that she didn't have a clue what Nigel or any other man was like in bed. And she'd certainly never been openly challenged on the subject before— especially by a man who was also a complete stranger.

She knew what happened physically, of course. She wasn't that much of a fool or an innocent. But she didn't know what to expect emotionally.

She hoped that loving Nigel would be enough, and that he would teach her the rest. It was quite some time since he'd made a serious attempt to get her into bed, she thought remorsefully. But she couldn't and wouldn't delay the moment any longer. It was long overdue.

Perhaps it was the fear of rejection which had kept him away so often lately. She'd been so wrapped up in her own life and its worries that she hadn't truly considered his feelings.

I've just been totally insensitive, she thought wearily. And the tragedy is that it took someone like Marc Delaroche to make me see it.

But from now on everything's going to be different, she promised herself firmly.

* * *

I still can't believe you're back already,' Lottie said, as she put a shepherd's pie in the oven. 'Your phone call gave me a real jolt. I wasn't expecting you until tomorrow at the earliest.' She threw Helen a searching glance over her shoulder. 'Didn't you meet up with Nigel?'

'Oh, yes,' Helen said brightly. 'We had an amazing lunch in one of the newest restaurants.'

'Lunch, eh?' Lottie pursed her lips. 'Now, I had you down for a romantic dinner *à deux*, then back to his place for a night of seething passion. Supper with me is a pretty dull alternative.'

Helen smiled at her. 'Honey, nothing involving you is ever dull. And, to be honest, I couldn't wait to get out of London.'

Lottie gave her a careful look as she sat down at the kitchen table and began to string beans. 'Your interview with the committee didn't go so well?'

Helen sighed. 'I honestly don't know. Most of them seemed pleasant and interested, but perhaps they were humouring me.'

'And is this Marc Delaroche guy that you phoned me about included in the 'pleasant and interested' category?' Lottie enquired.

'No,' Helen returned, teeth gritted. 'He is not.'

'How did I guess?' Lottie said wryly. 'Anyway, following your somewhat emotional request from the station, I looked him up on the net.'

'And he was there?'

'Oh, yes,' Lottie nodded. 'And he's into buildings.'

'An architect?' Helen asked, surprised.

'Not exactly. He's the chairman of Fabrication Roche, a company that makes industrial buildings—instant factories from kits, cheap and ultra-efficient, especially in developing countries. The company's won awards for the designs, and they've made him a multimillionaire.'

'Then what the hell is someone from that kind of background doing on a committee that deals with heritage projects?' Helen shook her head. 'It makes no sense.'

'Except he must know about costing,' Lottie pointed out

practically. 'And applying modern technology to restoration work. The others deal with aesthetics. He looks at the bottom line.'

Helen's lips tightened. 'Well, I hope the ghastly modern eye-sore we met in today wasn't a sample of his handiwork.'

'I wouldn't know about that.' Lottie grinned at her. 'But I've printed everything off for you to read at your leisure.' She paused. 'No photograph of him, I'm afraid.'

'It doesn't matter,' Helen said quietly. 'I already know what he looks like.'

And I know the way he looked at me, she thought, remembering her sense of helpless outrage as his gaze had moved over her body. And that glinting smile in his eyes...

She swallowed, clearing the image determinedly from her mind. 'But thanks for doing that, Lottie. It's always best to— know your enemy.'

'Even better not to have an enemy in the first place,' Lottie retorted, rinsing the beans in a colander. 'Especially one with his kind of money.' She went to the dresser to fetch a bottle of red wine and a corkscrew. 'Did you tell Nigel how your interview went?'

Helen hesitated. 'Some of it. He was really pushed for time, so I couldn't go into details.'

'And you'll be seeing him this weekend, no doubt?'

'Actually, no.' Helen made her voice sound casual. 'He's got a party to go to. A duty thing for his chairman's birthday.'

Lottie stared at her. 'And he hasn't asked you to go with him?' She sounded incredulous.

'Well, no,' Helen admitted awkwardly. 'But it's no big deal. It will be a black tie affair, and Nigel knows quite well I haven't anything to wear to something like that.' She gave a little laugh. 'He probably wanted to save me embarrassment.'

'For the same reason he might have considered buying you an evening dress,' Lottie said with a touch of curtness. 'He can certainly afford it.'

Helen shrugged. 'But he didn't,' she said. 'And it really

doesn't matter.' She paused. 'Of course it will be different when we're officially engaged.'

'I hope so,' Lottie agreed drily, filling their glasses.

'And what about you?' Helen was suddenly eager to change the subject. 'Have you heard from Simon?'

Her friend's face lit up, her blue eyes sparkling. 'The dam's nearly finished, and he's coming home on leave next month. Only two weeks, but that's better than nothing, and we're going to talk serious wedding plans. He says from now on he's only accepting contracts which allow accompanying wives, so I think he's missing me.'

Helen smiled at her teasingly. 'You can't leave,' she protested. 'How are the locals to give dinner parties without you to cook for them?'

'I promise I won't go before I cater for your wedding reception,' Lottie promised solemnly. 'So can you please fix a date?'

'I'll make it a priority,' Helen returned.

She was in a thoughtful mood when she walked home that night. There'd been a shower of rain about an hour before, and the air was heady with the scent of damp earth and sweet grass.

She was delighted at Lottie's obvious happiness, but at the same time unable to subdue a small pang of envy.

She wished her own life was falling so splendidly and lovingly into place.

Yet Nigel seems to be managing perfectly well without me, she thought sadly. If only we could have talked today—really talked—then maybe we'd have had Lottie's romantic kind of evening—and night—after all. And he'd have bought me a ring, and a dress, and taken me to Sussex. And he'd have told everyone, 'This is my brand-new fiancée. I simply couldn't bear to leave her behind.'

She'd started the day with such optimism and determination, yet now she felt uneasy and almost frightened. Nothing had gone according to plan. And miles away, in a glass and concrete box, her fate had probably already been decided.

I need Nigel, she thought. I need him to hold me and tell me everything will be all right, and that Monteagle is safe.

She walked under the arched gateway and stood in the courtyard, looking at the bulk of the house in the starlight. Half-seen, like this, it seemed massive—impregnable—but she knew how deceptive it was.

And it wasn't just her own future under threat. There were the Marlands, George and Daisy, who'd come to work for her grandfather when they were a young married couple, as gardener and cook respectively. As the other staff had left George had learned to turn his hand to more and more things about the estate, and his wife, small, cheerful and bustling, had become the housekeeper. Helen, working alongside them, depended on them totally, but knew unhappily that she could not guarantee their future—specially from Trevor Newson.

'Too old,' he'd said. 'Too set in their ways. I'll be putting in my own people.'

You'll be putting in no one, she'd told herself silently.

I wish I still felt as brave now, she thought, swallowing. But, even so, I'm not giving up the fight.

Monteagle opened to the public on Saturdays in the summer. Marion Lowell the Vicar's wife, who was a keen historian, led guided tours round the medieval ruins and those parts of the adjoining Jacobean house not being used as living accommodation by Helen and the Marlands.

Her grandfather had been forced to sell the books from his library in the eighties, and Helen now used the room as her sitting room. It had a wonderful view across the lawns to the lake, so the fact that it was furnished with bits and pieces from the attics, and a sofa picked up for a song at a house clearance sale a few miles away, was no real hardship.

If the weather was fine Helen and Daisy Marland served afternoon teas, with home-made scones and cakes, in the courtyard. With the promise of warm sunshine to come, they'd spent most of Friday evening baking.

Helen had been notified that a coach tour, travelling under the faintly depressing title 'Forgotten Corners of History' would be arriving mid-afternoon, so she'd got George to set up wooden trestles, covered with the best of the linen sheets, and flank them with benches.

Placing a small pot of wild flowers in the centre of each table, she felt reasonably satisfied, even if it was a lot of effort for very moderate returns. However, it was largely a goodwill gesture, and on that level it worked well. Entries in the visitors' book in the Great Hall praised the teas lavishly, particularly Daisy's featherlight scones, served with cream and home-made jam.

For once, the coach arrived punctually, and as one tour ended the next began. Business in the courtyard was brisk, but evenly spaced for a change, so they were never 'rushed to death', as Mrs Marland approvingly put it. The weather had lived up to the forecast, and although Monteagle closed officially at six, it was well after that when the last visitors reluctantly departed, prising themselves away from the warmth of the early-evening sun.

The clearing away done, Helen hung up the voluminous white apron she wore on these occasions, today over neatly pressed jeans and a blue muslin shirt, kicked off her sandals, and strolled across the lawns down to the edge of the lake. The coolness of the grass felt delicious under her aching soles, and the rippling water had its usual soothing effect.

If only every open day could go as smoothly, she thought dreamily.

Although that would not please Nigel, who had always made his disapproval clear. 'Working as a glorified waitress,' he'd said. 'What on earth do you think your grandfather would say?'

'He wouldn't say anything,' Helen had returned, slightly nettled by his attitude. 'He'd simply roll up his sleeves and help with the dishes.'

Besides, she thought, the real problem was Nigel's mother Celia, a woman who gave snobbishness a bad name. She liked the idea of Helen having inherited Monteagle, but thought it should have come with a full staff of retainers and a convenient treasure chest in the dungeon to pay the running costs, so she had little sympathy with Helen's struggles.

She sighed, moving her shoulders with sudden uneasiness

inside the cling of the shirt. Her skin felt warm and clammy, and she was sorely tempted to walk round to the landing stage beside the old boathouse, as she often did, strip off her top clothes and dive in for a cooling swim.

That was what the thought of Nigel's mother did to her, she told herself. Or was it?

Because she realised with bewilderment that she had the strangest sensation that someone somewhere was watching her, and that was what she found suddenly disturbing.

She swung round defensively, her brows snapping together, and realised with odd relief that it was only Mrs Lowell, coming towards her across the grass, wreathed in smiles.

'What a splendid afternoon,' she said, triumphantly rattling the cash box she was carrying. 'No badly behaved children for once, and we've completely sold out of booklets. Any chance of the wonderful Lottie printing off some more for us?'

'I mentioned we were getting low the other evening, and they'll be ready for next week.' Helen assured her, then paused. 'We have had a good crowd here today.' She gave a faint grin. 'The coach party seemed the usual motley crew, but docile enough.'

Mrs Lowell wrinkled her brow. 'Actually, they seemed genuinely interested. Not a hint of having woken up and found themselves on the wrong bus. They asked all sorts of questions—at least one of them did—and he gave me a generous tip at the end, which I've added to funds.'

'You shouldn't do that,' Helen reproved. 'Your tour commentaries are brilliant, and I only wish I could pay you. If someone else enjoys listening to you that much, then you should keep the money for yourself.'

'I love doing it,' Mrs Lowell told her. 'And it gets me out of the house while Jeff is writing his sermon,' she added conspiratorially. 'Apparently even a pin dropping can interrupt the creative flow. It's just as well Em's got a holiday job, because when she's around the house is in turmoil. And it's a good job, too, that she wasn't here to spot the coach party star,' she went on thoughtfully. 'You must have noticed him yourself during tea, Helen. Very dishy, in an unconventional way, and totally unmissable. What Em would describe as "sex on legs"—but not, I hope, in front of her father. He's still getting over the navel-piercing episode.'

Helen stared at her, puzzled. 'I didn't notice anyone within a hundred miles who'd answer to "dishy"—especially with the coach party. They all seemed well struck in years to me.' She grinned. 'Maybe he stayed away from tea because he felt eating scones and cream might damage his to-die-for image. Perhaps I should order in some champagne and caviar instead.'

'Maybe you should.' Mrs Lowell sighed. 'But what a shame you missed him. And he had this marvellous accent, too—French, I think.'

Helen nearly dropped the cash box she'd just been handed. She said sharply, 'French? Are you sure?'

'Pretty much.' The Vicar's wife nodded. 'Is something wrong, dear?'

'No—oh, no,' Helen denied hurriedly. 'It's just that we don't get many foreign tourists, apart from the odd American. It seems—strange, that's all.'

But that wasn't all, and she knew it. In fact it probably wasn't the half of it, she thought as they walked back to the house.

She always enjoyed this time after the house had closed, when they gathered in the kitchen to count the takings over a fresh pot of tea and the leftover cakes. And today she should have been jubilant. Instead she found herself remembering that sudden conviction that unseen eyes had been upon her by the lake, and it made her feel restive and uneasy—as well as seriously relieved that she hadn't yielded to her impulse by stripping off and diving in.

Of course there were plenty of French tourists in England, and their visitor might well turn out to be a complete stranger, but Helen felt that her encounter with Marc Delaroche in the Martinique had used up her coincidence quota for the foreseeable future.

It was him, she thought. It had to be…

As soon as Mrs Lowell had gone Helen dashed round to the

Great Hall and looked in the visitors' book, displayed on an impressive refectory table in the middle of the chamber.

She didn't have to search too hard. The signature 'Marc Delaroche' was the day's last entry, slashed arrogantly across the foot of the page.

She straightened, breathing hard as if she'd been running. He might have arrived unannounced, but his visit was clearly no secret. He wanted her to know about it.

She simply wished she'd known earlier. But there was no need to get paranoid about it, she reminded herself. He'd been here, seen Monteagle on a better than normal working day, and now he'd gone—without subjecting her to any kind of confrontation. So maybe he'd finally accepted that she wanted no personal connection between them, and from now on any encounters they might have would be conducted on strictly formal business lines.

And the fact they'd been so busy today, and their visitors had clearly enjoyed themselves, might even stand her in good stead when the time came for decisions to be made.

At any rate, that was how she intended to see the whole incident, she decided with a determined nod, then closed the book and went back to her own part of the house, locking up behind her.

Helen awoke early the next morning, aware that she hadn't slept as well as she should have done. She sometimes wished she could simply turn over and go back to sleep, letting worries and responsibilities slide into oblivion. But that simply wasn't possible. There was always too much to do.

Anyway, as soon as the faint mist cleared it was going to be another glorious day, she thought, pushing aside the bedcover and swinging her feet to the floor. And, as such days didn't come around that often, she didn't really want to miss a moment of it.

She decided she'd spend the day in the garden, helping George to keep the ever-encroaching weeds at bay. But first she'd cycle down to the village and get a paper. After all, they might finish the crossword, earn some money that way.

George was waiting for her as she rode back up the drive. 'All right, slave driver,' she called to him. 'Can't I even have a cup of coffee before you get after me?'

'I'll put your bike away, Miss Helen.' George came forward as she dismounted. 'Daisy came down just now to say you've a visitor waiting. Best not to keep him, she thought.'

Helen was suddenly conscious of an odd throbbing, and realised it was the thud of her own pulses. She ran the tip of her tongue round her dry mouth.

'Did Daisy say—who it was?' she asked huskily.

He shook his head. 'Just that it was someone for you, miss.'

She knew, of course, who it would be. Who it had to be, she thought, her lips tightening in dismay.

Her immediate impulse was to send George with a message that she hadn't returned yet and he didn't know when to expect her. But that wouldn't do. For one thing it would simply alarm Daisy and send her into search-party mode. For another it would tell her visitor that she was scared to face him, and give him an advantage she was reluctant to concede.

Surprised, cool, but civil, she decided. That was the route to take.

Of course there was always an outside chance that it could be Nigel, returned early from Sussex for some reason—because he was missing her, perhaps. But she couldn't really make herself believe it.

In a perverse way she hoped it wasn't Nigel, because she knew what she looked like in old jeans, with a polo shirt sticking damply to her body and her hair bundled into an untidy knot on top of her head and secured by a silver clip, and knew that he disliked seeing her like that.

But, no matter who was waiting for her, she owed it to herself and no one else to make herself slightly more presentable, even if it was only a matter of washing her face and hands and tidying her hair.

She supposed reluctantly that she'd better sneak in through the kitchen and go up the back stairs to her room.

But he'd forestalled her—the intruder—because he was already there in the kitchen, sitting at the table and tucking into a bacon sandwich with total relish while Daisy fussed round him, filling his cup with more coffee.

Helen halted abruptly. 'What are you doing here?' She heard the note of aggression in her voice and saw Daisy glance at her, her lips pursed.

Marc Delaroche got to his feet. In casual khaki pants and a short-sleeved black shirt, he looked less of a business tycoon and more of a tough from the back streets of Marseilles.

'As you see, *mademoiselle*, I am having some breakfast.' He slanted a smile at Daisy. 'Your housekeeper is an angel who has taken pity on me.'

Helen forced herself to amend her tone slightly. 'I meant surely you saw everything you needed to yesterday, so why are you still around?' She pushed a dusty strand of hair back from her face. 'After all, a village is hardly your kind of place.'

'I still had some unfinished business here,' he said softly. 'So I decided to spend the night at the Monteagle Arms.'

She raised her brows. 'They don't do breakfast?'

'Of course,' he said. 'But after the dinner they served last night I was not tempted to try the *petit dejeuner*.' He gestured at his plate. 'May I continue?'

'Coffee, Miss Helen?' Daisy placed another mug on the table and waited, coffeepot poised, her expression indicating that her employer had breached quite enough of the laws of hospitality already.

'Please.' Helen gave her a swift conciliatory smile, and subsided unwillingly on to the chair opposite him.

She was bitterly aware that she'd neglected to put on a bra that morning—a fact that would not be lost on her unwanted guest, she thought angrily, burning her mouth on an unwary gulp of coffee.

'You mentioned unfinished business?' she said after a pause. 'I presume it's something to do with the house?' She forced a smile. 'After all, why else would you be here?'

'Why indeed?' he agreed cordially.

'So…' Helen gestured awkwardly. 'If I can help…?'

'I was not able to see all the rooms in the house during the tour yesterday, because your charming guide told me they are the private living quarters of yourself and your staff.' Marc Delaroche paused. 'Perhaps you could show them to me presently?'

Helen put down her mug. 'Is that strictly necessary?'

'It is,' he said. 'Or I would not have asked. Your application to the committee covered the entire building, not merely selected sections, as I am sure you understand. And your accommodation includes rooms of historic importance—the library, I believe, and the Long Gallery, and also the State Bedroom.' He gave her an enquiring look. 'Is that where you sleep, perhaps?' He added gently, 'I hope you do not find the question indelicate.'

'I have never slept there,' Helen said coldly. 'It was last occupied by my grandfather, and I wasn't planning to make it available to the public.'

'Even though one of your kings used it for a romantic rendezvous? Charles the First, I think?'

'Charles the Second,' Helen corrected. 'He's supposed to have come here to seduce the daughter of the house, who'd fled from court to escape him.'

His brows lifted. 'And did he succeed in his quest?'

'I haven't the faintest idea,' Helen said shortly. 'And, anyway, it's just a legend. I don't believe a word of it even though I was named after her!'

'*Quel dommage,*' he murmured.

'Well, Sir Henry always said it was true,' Daisy interposed from the stove.

'My grandfather liked to tease people,' Helen said stonily. 'He said the room was haunted, too, if you remember.'

'And you thought if you slept there you might wake to find a ghost in your bed?' The dark eyes were dancing.

'Not at all,' Helen denied. 'I simply prefer my own room.'

'Until you are married, *hein*?' Marc Delaroche said carelessly. 'When you have a living man beside you at night, *ma belle*, there will be no room for ghosts.'

'Thank you,' Helen told him, biting her lip. 'You paint such a frank picture.'

He shrugged. 'Marriage is a frank relationship.' He paused.

'But, legend or not, the State Bedroom and its romantic associations should be available to your public. I hope you will allow me to be its first visitor.'

Helen finished her coffee. 'Just as you wish, *monsieur*. Would you like to begin now?'

'*Pourquoi pas?*' he said softly. 'Why not?'

Oh, Helen thought wearily as she led the way to the kitchen door, I can think of so many reasons why not. And having to be alone with you, Monsieur Delaroche, heads the list every time.

And, heaven help me, I'm not even sure whether it's you I don't trust—or myself.

CHAPTER THREE

HELEN was still recovering from that unwelcome piece of self-revelation when they entered the library together. She pushed her hands into the pockets of her jeans, trying to compose herself for the inevitable inquisition, but at first there was only silence as Marc Delaroche stood looking round with a frown at the empty oak shelves that still lined the walls.

'It was a valuable collection?' he asked at last.

'Yes—very.' She hesitated. 'My grandfather was forced to sell it in the eighties, along with a number of pictures. It almost broke his heart, but it gave Monteagle a reprieve.'

He shook his head slightly, his gaze travelling over the motley collection of shabby furniture, the peeling paintwork, and the ancient velvet curtains hanging limply at the windows. 'And this is where you spend your leisure time?'

'Yes, what there is of it,' she returned. 'There's always some job needing to be done in a place like this.'

'You do not find it—*triste*? A little gloomy.'

'In winter it's quite cosy,' she retorted defensively. 'There's plenty of wood on the estate, so I have an open fire, and I burn candles most of the time.'

'Certainly a kinder light than a midsummer sun,' he commented drily. 'Shall we continue?'

She supposed they must. The truth was she felt totally unnerved by her physical consciousness of his presence beside her. Although he was deliberately keeping his distance, she realised, and standing back to allow her to precede him through doorways, and up the Great Staircase to the Long Gallery. But it made no difference. The panelled walls still seemed to press in upon them, forcing them closer together. An illusion, she knew, but no less disturbing for that.

She thought, I should have made some excuse—asked Daisy to show him round.

Aloud, she said, 'This is where the family used to gather, and where the ladies of the house took exercise in bad weather.'

'But not, of course, with holes in the floorboards,' he said.

She bit her lip. 'No. The whole floor needs replacing, including the joists.'

He was pausing to look at the portraits which still hung on the walls. 'These are members of your family? Ancestors?'

She pulled a face. 'Mostly the ugly ones that my grandfather thought no one would buy.'

Marc Delaroche slanted an amused look at her, then scanned the portraits again. 'Yet I would say it is the quality of the painting that is at fault.'

She shrugged, surprised at his perception. 'No, they're not very good. But I guess you didn't pay the fees of someone like Joshua Reynolds to paint younger sons and maiden aunts.'

'And so the sons went off, *sans doute*, to fight my countrymen in some war,' he commented, his mouth twisting. 'While the aunts had only to remain maiden. My sympathies are with them, I think.' He paused. 'Is there no portrait of the beauty so desired by King Charles?'

'Yes,' she admitted reluctantly. 'My grandfather wouldn't part with it. It's in the State Bedroom.'

'I cannot wait,' he murmured. *En avant, ma belle.*'

'Do you mind not calling me that?' Helen threw over her shoulder as they set off again. 'What would you say if I greeted you with, Hey, good-looking?'

'I should advise you to consult an eye specialist,' he said drily. 'Tell me something, *mademoiselle*. Why do you object when a man indicates he finds you attractive?'

'I don't,' she said shortly. 'When it's the right man.'

'And I am by definition the wrong one?' He sounded amused.

'Do you really need to ask? You know already that I'm engaged to be married.'

'Of course,' he said. 'But where is your fiancé?'

'He couldn't come down this weekend.' Helen halted, chin lifted in challenge. 'Not that it's any concern of yours.'

'This weekend?' he said musingly. 'And how many weekends before that? It is a matter of comment in the village, you understand.'

'The public bar of the Monteagle Arms anyway,' Helen said tersely. 'You really shouldn't listen to idle gossip, *monsieur*.'

'But I learned a great deal,' Marc Delaroche said gently. 'And not merely about your missing lover. They spoke too about your fight to keep this house. Opinion is divided as to whether you are brave or a fool, but none of them thought you could win.'

'How kind of them,' she said between her teeth. 'That must have done my cause a lot of good.' She paused. 'Did they know who you were—and why you were here?'

'I said nothing. I only listened.' He shrugged. 'They spoke of your grandfather with affection, but not of your parents. And you do not mention them either. I find that strange.'

Helen bit her lip. 'I hardly knew them. They left Britain when I was still quite small, and my grandfather brought me up with the help of various nannies. That's why we were so close.'

Marc Delaroche frowned swiftly. 'My father's work took him abroad also, but I travelled with him always. He would never have considered anything else.'

'My father didn't work—in the accepted sense.' Helen looked past him, staring into space. 'He'd been brought up to run Monteagle and the estate, but after the financial disasters we'd suffered that no longer seemed an option. Also, he knew he would never have a son to inherit what remained. My mother, whom he adored, was very ill when I was born, and needed an immediate operation. The name was going to die out.'

'He had a daughter. Did he not consider that?'

Helen's smile was swift and taut. 'I never had the chance to ask him. There's always been a strong gambling streak in our family—fortunes won and lost down the centuries—and my father was a brilliant poker player. He had a load of friends among the rich and famous, so he travelled the world with my mother, staying in other people's houses and making a living from cards and backgammon.' Her mouth twisted wryly. 'At times he even earned enough to send money home.'

'But then his luck ran out?' Marc Delaroche asked quietly.

She nodded, and began to walk along the corridor again. 'They were in the Caribbean, flying between islands in a private plane with friends. There was some problem, and the aircraft crashed into the sea, killing everyone on board. My grandfather was devastated. Up to then he'd always believed we would recoup our losses somehow, and carry out the restoration work he'd always planned. That we'd be reunited as a family, too. But after the crash the fight seemed to go out of him. He became—resigned. Instead of winning, he talked about survival.'

She stared ahead of her, jaw set. 'But Monteagle is mine now, and I want more than that.'

'Has it hurt you to tell me these things?' His voice was oddly gentle.

'It's all part of Monteagle's history.' She hunched a shoulder. 'So you probably have a right to ask. But that's as far as the personal details go,' she added, giving him a cool look. 'You're here on business, and I feel we should conduct ourselves in a businesslike manner.'

Oh, God, she groaned inwardly. Just listen to yourself. Miss Prim of the Year, or what?

'Ah,' he said. 'And therefore all matters of gender should be rigorously excluded?' His grin was cynical. 'How do you do that, I wonder?'

She bit her lip. 'That is your problem, *monsieur*. Not mine.'

She reached the imposing double doors at the end of the corridor and flung them open. 'And here, as you requested, is the State Bedroom.'

The curtains were half drawn over the long windows, and she walked across and opened them, admitting a broad shaft of dust-filled sunshine.

It was a big room, the walls hung with faded brocade wallpaper. It was dominated by the huge four-poster bed, which had been stripped to its mattress, although the heavily embroidered satin canopy and curtains were still in place.

'As you see,' she added woodenly, 'it has not been in use since my grandfather died.' She pointed to a door. 'That leads to a dressing room, which he always planned to convert to a bathroom.'

Her companion gave it a cursory glance. 'It is hardly big enough. One would need to include the room next door as well.'

'Just for a bath? Why?'

He grinned lazily at her. 'A leading question, *ma mie*. Do you really wish me to enlighten you.'

'No,' she said. 'Thank you.'

Marc Delaroche took a longer look around him, then walked over to the fireplace and studied the picture hung above it. The girl in it looked steadily, even a little shyly back at him, a nimbus of warm-toned ringlets surrounding her face. She was wearing pale yellow satin, cut decorously for the fashion of the time. There was a string of pearls round her throat, and she carried a golden rose in one hand.

He whistled softly. 'I wonder how long she fought before she surrendered to your king?' he said, half to himself.

'You think she did surrender?'

'Eventually. As all women must,' he returned, ignoring her small outraged gasp. 'Besides, there is no question. You have only to look at her mouth.' He held out an imperative hand. '*Viens.*'

In spite of herself, Helen found she was crossing the worn carpet and standing at his side. 'What are you talking about?'

'She is trying hard to be the virtuous lady, but her lips are parted and the lower one is full, as if swollen from the kiss she longs for.'

'I think you have a vivid imagination, *monsieur*,' Helen retorted, her voice slightly strained.

'And I think that you also, *mademoiselle*, are trying much too hard.' His voice sank almost to a whisper.

Before she could guess his intention and move away, out of range, Marc Delaroche lifted a hand and put his finger to her own mouth, tracing its curve in one swift breathless movement, then allowing his fingertip delicately to penetrate her lips and touch the moist inner heat.

In some strange way it would have been less intimate—less shocking—if he'd actually kissed her.

She gasped and stepped backwards, the blaze in her eyes meeting the mockery in his. Her words became chips of ice. 'How dare you—touch me?'

'A conventional response,' he said. 'I am disappointed.'

'You're going to have more than disappointment to deal with, Monsieur Delaroche. You'll live to regret this, believe me.' She drew a deep breath. 'Because I, too, shall be making a report to your committee, informing them how you've abused their trust while you've been here, conducting enquiries on their behalf. And I hope they fire you—no matter how much money you have,' she added vindictively.

'I am desolate to tell you this, but you are in error, *ma belle*,' he drawled. 'The committee is not concerned with my visit. It was my decision alone to come here.'

She looked at him, stunned. 'But—you've asked all these questions…'

He shrugged. 'I was curious. I wished to see this house that means so much to you.'

The breath caught suddenly, painfully in her throat. She turned and marched to the door, and held it open. 'And now the tour is over. So please leave. Now.'

'But that was not all.' He made no attempt to move. 'I came most of all because I wanted to see you again. And ask you something.'

'Ask it,' Helen said curtly. 'Then get out.'

He said softly, 'Will you sleep with me tonight?'

Helen was rigid, staring at him with widening eyes. When she could speak, she said hoarsely, 'I think you must have taken leave of your senses.'

'Not yet,' he drawled. His eyes went over her body in lingering, sensuous assessment. 'For that I shall have to wait a little, I think.'

She pressed her hands to the sudden flare of hot blood in her face.

'How dare you speak to me like this?' she whispered jerkily. 'Insult me in this way?'

'Where is the insult? I am telling you that I desire you, and have done since the first moment I saw you. And please do not insult me by pretending you did not know,' he added silkily, 'because I did not hide it.'

It seemed altogether wiser to ignore that. Helen struggled to control her breathing. 'You—you seem to have forgotten that I'm about to marry another man.'

'He is the one who has forgotten, *ma belle*,' he said, a touch of grimness in his voice.

'And you imagined that because he's not here I would turn to you for—consolation?' Her voice rose. 'Oh, God—how dare you? What do you take me for? I love Nigel, and I intend to belong to him and no one else. And I'll wait for him for ever if necessary. Not that someone like you could ever understand that,' she added, her voice ringing with contempt.

There was an odd silence as he studied her, eyes narrowed. Then, 'You are wrong, *ma mie*,' he said softly. '*Parce que, enfin, je comprends tout.*' He gave a brief, harsh sigh. 'I see I shall have to be patient with you, Hélène, but my ultimate reward will make it worthwhile.'

'Damn you,' she said violently. 'Can't you see I'd die rather than let you touch me again?'

He reached her almost before she had finished speaking, and pulled her against him, crushing the breath from her as his lips descended on hers.

Nothing in her life had prepared her for the heated relentlessness of his kiss, and he took all the time he needed, exploring deeply, draining every drop of sweetness from her startled mouth.

Tiny fires were dancing in the dark eyes when, at last, he released her.

'You see,' he told her ironically, 'you still live. So learn from this, and do not issue ridiculous challenges that you cannot hope to win.' He took her hand and raised it to his mouth, palm uppermost, and she cried out in shock as his teeth grazed the soft mound beneath her thumb.

'*Au revoir, ma belle,*' he said softly. 'And remember this— on my next visit I shall expect to spend the night.'

And he left her standing there, mute and shaken as she stared after him, her tingling hand pressed to her startled, throbbing mouth.

A lot of those weeds you're pulling out are plants, Miss Helen,' George told her reproachfully.

Helen jumped guiltily, looking at the wilted greenery in her trug. 'Oh, Lord,' she said dismally. 'I'm sorry.'

She'd hoped that some intensive gardening would calm her down and restore her equilibrium, but it wasn't working out like that.

The thought of Marc Delaroche was interfering with her concentration at every level, and this infuriated her.

She had tried to call Nigel and beg him to come down, even if it was only for a couple of hours, so she could talk to him. But his mobile phone was permanently switched off, it seemed.

And even if she had managed to contact him, what could she have said? That she needed him to hold her and kiss her and take away the taste of another man's mouth?

The only other man, in fact, who had ever kissed her in passion.

Her mouth still seemed swollen and faintly tingling from the encounter, but maybe she was just being paranoid. Someone had made a pass at her, that was all. The sort of thing that she should have been able to take in her stride if she'd possessed an ounce of sophistication. She could even have laughed about it, telling Nigel, You'd better stake your claim, darling, because I'm being seriously fancied by someone else.

And he would have laughed too, because he knew she'd never looked at anyone but him since she was thirteen, and that they belonged together.

Anyway, her best plan would be to put the whole thing out of her mind. Marc Delaroche had simply been amusing himself, she thought, and he probably had his next target already lined up. Quite apart from his admittedly diabolical attraction, he was rich enough to ensure that he didn't get many refusals. And he wouldn't waste time repining over any of the few women who resisted him. Or risk another rejection by returning.

He'd called her *'ma belle'*, but that had to be just a seduction ploy, because she wasn't beautiful at all. Moderately attractive was the best she could honestly claim, and he knew it. He'd probably thought she would fall into his arms through sheer gratitude, she told herself, viciously slicing her trowel through a dandelion root.

All the same, she wished desperately that he hadn't sought her out and forced this confrontation on her.

She might not like him, and she certainly didn't trust him, but she could have done with him on her side when the committee came to make their decision.

No chance of that now, of course. And she still couldn't understand what had possessed him. Yes, she'd been aware of him too, she admitted defensively, but only because she'd had no choice. During the interview he'd hardly taken his eyes off her. But she certainly hadn't offered him any encouragement to—pursue her like this. Quite the opposite, in fact.

At the same time she felt oddly depressed. She absolutely didn't want him as a lover. She probably wouldn't choose him as a friend, but she surely didn't need him as an enemy either, she thought, and sighed without quite knowing why.

The sun went down that evening behind a bank of cloud, and the following day brought grey skies and drizzle and the temperature dropping like a stone.

Outside work had to be halted, and if the miserable conditions persisted to the weekend, the tourists would stay away too, Helen fretted.

She caught up on the household accounts—a depressing task at the best of times—helped Daisy bake for the freezer, and waited feverishly for the mail van to call each day. The committee chairman had said she would hear before the end of the month, and that was fast approaching. All she could hope was that no news might be good news.

Thankfully, Marc Delaroche had made no attempt to contact her again. Maybe he'd decided to cut his losses and retire from the fray after all. But the thought of him still made her uneasy, and her attempts to blot him from her memory did not appear to be working too well.

It would have made things so much easier if she'd been able to talk to Nigel, she acknowledged unhappily. But there'd been no reply from his flat after the weekend, so she'd gritted her teeth and made the unpopular move of phoning him at work—only to be told that he was working in Luxembourg all week. And when she'd asked for the name of his hotel, she'd been told briskly that the bank did not give out that sort of information.

Back to square one, she realised without pleasure. Unless he called her instead, of course, and how likely was that?

She stopped herself right there. She was being critical, which was only one step removed from disloyal. Especially when she knew from past experience that these trips were often landed on him at ridiculously short notice. And he was bound to be home at the weekend, she told herself, because this time it was his mother's birthday.

Helen didn't know what kind of celebration was being planned, but she'd managed to find a card with a Persian cat on it that was the double of the bad-tempered specimen occupying its own special chair in Mrs Hartley's drawing room. She'd signed it 'Best wishes' rather than 'Love from', in tacit acknowledgement that her relationship with Nigel's mother had always been tricky. That was one of the reasons they'd delayed making their engagement official.

'She'll be fine,' Nigel had said. 'She just needs a bit of time to get used to the idea. And to you.'

But she's known me since I was thirteen, Helen had thought, troubled. And even then I don't think I was ever on her A-list.

Thought it—but hadn't said it.

Still, Mrs Hartley's sensibilities couldn't be allowed to intrude any longer—or any further. Helen suspected she was the kind of mother, anyway, who believed no girl would ever be good enough for her only son. Nothing useful would be achieved by putting off the announcement any longer.

Because, whether the committee's decision was for or against the restoration of Monteagle, she was going to need Nigel's love and support as never before. And surely, in spite of the demands of his career, he would understand that and be there for her—wouldn't he?

It irked her to realise that Marc Delaroche, however despicable his motives, had actually taken more interest in the house than Nigel had ever shown. And he was right about the State Bedroom, too. Her grandfather wouldn't have wanted it left untouched, like some empty shrine.

Instead, it should be top of her refurbishment list and opened to the public. She might find the Charles the Second legend distasteful, but a lot of people would think it a romantic story, and let their imaginations free on the use that giant four-poster had been put to during the King's visit.

She went up there with a notebook and pen and took a clear-eyed look round. The ornamental plaster on the ceiling was in urgent need of restoration in places, and there were timbered walls waiting to be exposed underneath layers of peeling wallpaper. The ancient Turkish carpet was past praying for, but it was concealing wooden floorboards that the original surveyor's report had declared free of woodworm or dry rot, and she could only hope that was still the case.

The silk bed hangings and window curtains were frankly disintegrating, and couldn't be saved, but their heavy embroidery was intact, and still beautiful.

Helen recalled that Mrs Stevens at the village post office, who was a skilled needlewoman, had told her months ago that if the elaborate patterns were cut out carefully they could be transferred to new fabric. She'd suggested, too, that the embroidery group at the Women's Institute, which she chaired, might take it on as a project.

First catch your fabric, Helen thought, doing some rueful calculations. But at least she knew now what her first priority should be, even though it was galling that she'd been alerted to it by Marc Delaroche.

But if I get the money from the committee I might even feel marginally grateful to him, she thought. Maybe.

She was sitting at the kitchen table on Friday evening, going over some of the estimates her grandfather had obtained and trying to work out the inevitable percentage increases for the intervening period, when Lottie arrived with the new batch of guidebooks.

'Hey, there.' She gave Helen a quizzical glance. 'Got any good news for me?'

'Not yet.' Helen gave a sigh. 'And I was so sure I'd hear this week.'

'Actually,' Lottie said, 'I was thinking of something more personal than the grant application.' She looked around. 'All on your own?' she enquired, with clear disappointment.

'Not any more.' Helen pushed her papers aside and got up to fill the kettle. 'Who were you expecting?'

'I thought Nigel might be here and had my speedy exit all planned,' Lottie explained. 'So—where is he?'

Helen shrugged as she got down the coffee jar. 'Arriving tomorrow, I guess. I haven't heard yet.'

Lottie frowned. 'But his car was in the drive at his parents' place earlier. That's when I put two and two together about the party.'

Helen stared at her. 'Lottie—what on earth are you talking about?'

'Oh, hell,' her friend groaned. 'Don't tell me I've put my foot in it. I was so sure…' She took a deep breath. 'It's just that Ma Hartley rang me this afternoon, all sweetness and light, wanting me to quote for catering a 'very special buffet' next month. She was so pleased and coy about it that I jumped to the obvious conclusion. I'm so sorry, love.'

Helen spooned coffee into two beakers with more than usual care. 'Nigel's probably planning it as a big surprise for me,' she said calmly, ignoring the sudden churning in her stomach. 'Although I can't really imagine his mother turning cartwheels over it. She must like me better than I thought,' she added, without any real conviction.

'I shouldn't have said anything,' Lottie said ruefully as she stirred her coffee.

'No, it's fine,' Helen assured her. 'And when I do see him I swear I'll be the world's most astonished person.'

That would be an easy promise to keep, she thought, when Lottie had gone. She was already bewildered and disturbed by his failure to contact her when he must know how she was longing to see him.

Well, she could do something about that at least, she thought, and she dialled the number of his parents' home.

She'd hoped Nigel himself would answer, but inevitably it was his mother.

'Oh, Helen,' she said, without pleasure. 'I'm afraid this isn't a terribly convenient moment. You see, we have guests, and we're in the middle of dinner.'

'I'm sorry,' Helen said. 'But I do need to speak to him.'

'But not this evening.' There was a steely note in Mrs Hartley's voice. She sighed impatiently. 'Oh, well. Perhaps if there's something particular, he could call you tomorrow?'

Oh, nothing special, thought Helen. Only the rest of my life.

'Thank you,' she said quietly. 'I look forward to hearing from him.'

But it wasn't true, she realised as she put down the phone. She had a feeling of dread, not anticipation. And once again Nigel's mother had succeeded in making her feel excluded— as if she had no place in their lives.

When she and Nigel finally managed to talk, Mrs Hartley's attitude was going to be one of the topics of conversation, she thought grimly.

When she awoke next morning, it was to intermittent sunshine and scudding clouds driven by a sharp breeze.

Unpredictable, she thought as she dressed. Rather like my life. But a good day for touring historic houses rather than going to the beach, so let's hope the queues start forming like they did last week.

Well, not quite, she amended hastily. At least this time Marc Delaroche would not be part of them.

She was on her way to the kitchen when she saw the post

van disappearing down the drive. At the door she paused, and drew a deep, calming breath before entering.

'Any phone calls for me?' she enquired, making her tone deliberately casual.

'Nothing so far,' Daisy told her, putting a fresh pot of tea on the table.

'What about mail?'

'A couple of bills,' Daisy said. She paused. 'And this.' She held out an imposing cream envelope embossed with the committee's logo.

Helen's stomach lurched frantically. She wiped her hand on her jeans and took the envelope, staring down at it. Reluctant, now that the moment had come, to learn its contents, slowly she pushed the blade of a table knife under the flap and slit it open.

The words 'We regret' danced in front of her eyes, making it almost unnecessary to read on. But she scanned them anyway—the brief polite lines that signified failure.

George had come into the kitchen and was standing beside his wife, both of them watching Helen anxiously.

She tried to smile—to shrug. 'No luck, I'm afraid. They try to help places that have suffered some kind of terrible devastation, like earthquake sites. It seems that rising damp, leaky roofs and dry rot aren't quite devastating enough.'

'Oh, Miss Helen, love.'

She sank her teeth into her lower lip at the compassion in Daisy's voice, forbidding herself to cry.

'Does this mean you'll have to sell to that Mr Newson?' George asked, troubled.

'No,' she said. 'I'm not going to do that. I'm never going to do that.' There was something else in the envelope, too. A note in the chairman's own hand, she discovered, wishing her well. 'Mr VanStratten and Monsieur Delaroche argued very persuasively on your behalf,' the note added, 'but eventually it had to be a majority decision.'

Her hand clenched round the paper, crushing it. That—lecherous hypocrite, speaking up for her? she thought incredulously. Dear God, that had to be the final blow.

Aloud, she said, 'There'll be something else I can do. Someone else I can turn to. I'll call Nigel. Ask for his advice.'

'He hasn't been so helpful up to now,' George muttered.

'But now the chips are down,' Helen said with more confidence than she actually felt. 'He'll find some way to rescue us.'

Rather than run the gauntlet of his mother's disapproval again, Helen rang Nigel's mobile number.

'Yes?' His voice sounded wary.

'Nigel?' she said. 'Darling, can you come round, please? I really need to see you.'

There was a silence, then he said, 'Look, Helen, this isn't a good time for me.'

'I'm sorry to hear that, but please believe that it's a far worse one for me,' she told him bluntly. 'Something's happened, and I need your advice.' She paused. 'Would you prefer me to come to you instead?'

'No,' he said hastily. 'No, don't do that. I'll be about half an hour, and I'll use the side gate into the garden. I'll meet you by the lake.'

'Bringing your cloak and dagger with you, no doubt,' Helen said acidly. 'But if that's what you want, then it's fine with me.'

She'd spoken bravely, but she rang off feeling sick and scared. Suddenly her entire life seemed to be falling in pieces, and she didn't know why, or how to deal with it.

Whatever, facing Nigel in working clothes wasn't a good idea. She dashed upstairs and took another quick shower, this time using the last of her favourite body lotion. From her scanty wardrobe she chose a straight skirt in honey-coloured linen, with a matching jersey top, long-sleeved and vee-necked.

She brushed her hair loose and applied a touch of pale rose to her mouth.

War paint, she thought ironically, as she took a last look in the mirror.

Nigel was already waiting when she arrived at the lakeside. The breeze across the water was ruffling his hair and he was pacing up and down impatiently.

'So there you are,' he greeted her peevishly. 'What the hell's the matter?'

'I think that should be my question.' She halted a few feet away, staring at him. 'You don't tell me you're coming down, and then you avoid me. Why?'

His eyes slid away uncomfortably. 'Look, Helen—I know I should have spoken before, but there's no easy way to say this.' He paused. 'You must know that things haven't been good between us for quite a while.'

'I've certainly realised we don't see as much of each other, but I thought it was pressure of work. That's what you told me, anyway.' She clenched her shaking hands and hid them in the folds of her skirt.

'And what about you?' he asked sharply. 'Always fussing about that decrepit ruin you live in—scratching round for the next few pennies. You've had a good offer for it. Why not wise up and get out while it's still standing?'

She gasped. 'How can you say that—when you know what it means to me?'

'Oh, I know all right,' he said bitterly. 'No one knows better. I discovered a long time ago I was always going to play second fiddle to that dump, and you took it for granted that I'd settle for that. No doubt that's what you want to talk about now. What's happened? Deathwatch beetle on the march again?'

'I do have a serious problem about the house, but that can wait,' she said steadily. 'What we obviously need to discuss is—us.'

'Helen, there is no 'us', and there hasn't been for a long time. But you refuse to see it, for some reason.'

Her nails dug painfully into the palms of her hands. 'Maybe because I'm in love with you.'

'Well, you've got a weird idea of what love's about,' Nigel commented sourly. 'Frankly, I'm sick and tired of this 'hands off till we're married' garbage. I've tried everything to get you into bed, but you've never wanted to know.'

She bit her lip. 'I—I realise that now, and I—I'm sorry.' She looked at him pleadingly. 'I thought you were prepared to wait too.'

'No,' he said brutally. 'Men only beg for so long, then they lose interest.' He shook his head. 'There's only ever going to be one passion in your life, Helen, and that's Monteagle. No guy stands a chance against a no-win obsession like that.'

She said carefully, 'You mean—you don't want me any more?'

He sighed. 'Let's be honest. It was a boy-girl thing at best, and it certainly didn't make it into the grown-up world. Although I hope we can stay friends,' he added hastily. 'Face it, you've never been interested in sex—or even curious. A couple of kisses have always been enough for you. But now I've met someone with a bit of warmth about her and we're getting married. I brought her down this weekend to meet my parents, so I really don't need you ringing up every five minutes.'

'I see.' Helen swallowed. 'You know, I had the strangest idea I was engaged to you myself.'

He shrugged. 'I know we discussed it,' he said awkwardly. 'But there was nothing definite. For one thing, I'd have had a hell of a fight on with my parents.'

'Oh, yes,' Helen said unevenly. 'I always knew they didn't like me.'

'It wasn't that,' he told her defensively. 'They felt we were wrong for each other, that's all. And they didn't want me tipping everything I earned down that money pit of yours, either.'

He paused. 'I have ambition, Helen, and I'm not ashamed of it. I want a wife who can help with my career—someone who likes entertaining and can provide the right ambience. Let's face it, you'd hate that kind of life.'

The wind was cold suddenly—turning her to ice.

She said quietly, 'And I haven't any money—to make up for my other deficiencies. Isn't that part of it?'

He gave her an irritated look. 'Money matters. Are you pretending it doesn't?'

'No,' she said. 'Particularly when I've just been turned down for my grant.'

'Well, what did you expect? Clearly they don't want to

throw good money after bad,' he said. 'That's not good business practice.'

She winced painfully. 'Nigel,' she said urgently, 'I—I'm trying to save the home I love. I thought you might be able to suggest something—someone who could help. Who might be prepared to invest in the estate...'

'This is a joke—right?' His tone was derisive. 'I suggest you look round for a rich husband—if you can find someone as frigid as you are yourself. And how likely is that?'

The pain was suddenly more than she could bear. She took a step towards him, lifting her hand, driven by a half-crazy need to wipe the sneer from his face.

Nigel retreated, throwing up an arm to ward her off, his smart brogues slipping suddenly in the mud created by the recent bad weather.

Helen saw his face change from alarm to fury as he overbalanced, teetering on the edge of the lake for a moment before he fell backwards into the water with a resounding splash.

He was on his feet instantly, dripping and crimson with rage. 'Bitch,' he shouted hoarsely, as Helen turned her back and began to walk, head bent, towards the house. 'Bitch.'

She was trembling violently, her breathing an agony, every nerve in her body striving to continue putting one foot in front of another so that she could reach sanctuary before she fell on her knees and howled her hurt and misery to the sky.

She was too blinded by his cruelty even to see that someone was standing in front of her until she collided with a hard male body and recoiled with a cry.

'Tais toi,' Marc Delaroche said quietly. 'Be calm.' His arm round her was like iron, holding her up. 'I have you safe. Now, walk with me to the house.'

And, too numb to resist, Helen could only obey.

CHAPTER FOUR

HE'D said 'walk', but Helen was dazedly aware she was being half-led, half-carried into the house. Warmth surrounded her, and a feeling of safety as its walls closed round her.

She heard Daisy's shocked exclamation, and his quiet reply.

When she could think clearly again she found she was sitting on the sofa in the library, with a mug of strong, hot tea clasped in her icy hands.

Marc Delaroche was standing by the fireplace, an elbow resting on the mantelshelf, looking contemplatively into the blue flames of the small twig fire that she supposed he'd kindled in the grate.

He was wearing jeans and a matching blue shirt, its top buttons undone and the sleeves rolled back, revealing the shadowing of dark hair on his chest and forearms.

He turned his head slowly and met her accusing gaze.

She said huskily, 'You knew, didn't you? I mean about Nigel. Somehow, you knew.'

There was a pause, then reluctantly he nodded. 'I regret, but, yes.'

'And is that why you're here—to gloat?' She took a gulp of the scalding brew in her beaker.

'No,' he said. 'Why should I do that?'

'Who knows,' she said, 'why you do anything? Yet here you are—again.'

'Among other things, I came to warn you. But I was too late.'

'How can this be?' Helen said, half to herself. 'How can you have guessed that Nigel didn't love me when I was still in the dark about it?'

He shrugged. 'You were in the dark, *ma mie*, because you had closed your eyes to what was happening—perhaps delib-

56

erately. Also,' he added, 'I had an advantage, because you were not sitting in the window of the Martinique that day when your supposed fiancé arrived. He came by taxi, not alone, and his companion was most reluctant to let him go. That was how I came to notice him—because their leavetaking was quite a spectacle. Each time he tried to say *au revoir* she wound herself round him the more. She behaved with *une ardeur etonnante*,' he added with a faint whistle. 'I almost envied him.'

He paused. 'And then I watched him join you at your table, and realised who he must be, and it was no longer so amusing.'

'So you took pity on me,' Helen said bitterly.

'Perhaps,' he said. 'But for a moment only. Because I could see that you were strong and would survive your disappointment.'

'Disappointment?' she echoed in angry incredulity. 'My God, I've just been dumped by the man I've loved all my life. The only man I'll ever love. And you talk about it as if it were a minor inconvenience.'

She paused. 'Why didn't you tell me there and then?'

'Because I already knew that the committee's decision would go against you,' he said. 'I did not wish to overburden you with bad news.'

'So instead you let me stew in my fool's paradise,' she said. 'Thank you so much.'

'Shall we agree it was a no-win situation for us both?' he suggested.

'I don't believe this,' Helen said raggedly. 'My life's in ruins, I'm falling apart—and you sound so bloody casual.'

She gave him an inimical look. 'And, for the record, there is no "both". There's myself alone, and no one else.'

'Are you so sure of that?'

'What are you saying? That he'll dump this new lady too, and come back to me?' She shook her head. 'I don't think so. And do you know why that is, Monsieur Delaroche? It's because I lack the necessary social skills. Also, I'm frigid—and she isn't,' she added, her voice cracking. Then stopped, horrified at what she'd let him see.

'He told you that?' Marc Delaroche raised his eyebrows. 'But how can he possibly know?'

She stared at him in silence, almost paralysed with shame as she interpreted what he'd just said to her. Oh God, she thought, he—he *knows* I'm still a virgin. And I wish I'd died before he told me so.

But you were the one who told *him*, said a small cold voice in her head. You let it slip the last time he was here. And *he* said he'd be patient. How could you have forgotten that?

She'd tried to block out every detail of their previous encounter, but that was something she should have remembered. Because it spelled danger.

'I understand now why you pushed him into the lake,' Marc added.

'I didn't push him,' Helen said icily. 'He slipped.'

'*Quel dommage,*' he murmured. 'And, no—he will certainly not come back,' he went on calmly. 'But for a reason far removed from the ones you have given.'

She said, 'Oh?' her voice wooden.

The dark eyes studied her. 'He did not tell you, *peut-être*, the identity of his new fiancée? Then I shall. Her name is Amanda Clayburn.'

'Clayburn?' Helen repeated, bewildered. 'You—you mean she's related to Sir Donald Clayburn, the chairman of the bank?'

'His only daughter.' His grin was cynical. 'Your Nigel is an ambitious man, *ma mie*. He has chosen money and the fast track to the boardroom.'

'No,' she said. 'He couldn't. He *wouldn't*. And, anyway, he doesn't need to do that. He has money of his own.'

'Which he prefers to keep, *sans doute*.' He bent and added another handful of twigs to the fire. 'But it is all true. I have a colleague with contacts at the bank, and he informs me their *affaire* has been an open secret for weeks. She is wild and spoiled, this Amanda, and her father, they say, is glad she is marrying before she disgraces him openly.'

'Obviously a marriage made in heaven.' The words cut at her, but she refused to wince. Instead, she threw back her head.

'Monteagle and Nigel—the two things I care most about in the world—I've lost them both.'

'I notice,' he said, 'you place the house before your fiancé.'

'Yes,' she said. 'Nigel said that too. He said that because of Monteagle I would never be capable of loving anyone properly. All in all, it was a pretty comprehensive condemnation. And do you know the worst of it, Monsieur Delaroche? You—you were here to watch it happening.' She almost choked on the words. 'You—of all the people in the world. You're like some terrible jinx—do you know that?—because each time you appear in my life, everything goes wrong.'

She punched her fist into the palm of her other hand. 'Well, you've had your fun, *monsieur*, if that's what you came for, so now you can go. I need to be on my own. Even you should be able to appreciate that,' she added burningly.

His own glance was cool. 'You have a strange idea of how I choose to amuse myself, *ma chère*,' he drawled. 'And, although I am desolate to grieve you further, I must tell you I have no intention of leaving yet. Because I came not just to warn you, but also to offer my help.'

'Oh, of course,' she said. 'You spoke up for me at the committee—you and your Dutch colleague. I—I suppose I should thank you.'

'If we had succeeded, perhaps,' he said. 'But as matters stand I do not expect you to torture yourself with an attempt to be grateful.'

'But why should you do that?' she asked. 'When you knew what the verdict would be? You don't look like someone who supports lost causes.'

He shrugged. 'Perhaps I felt you did not deserve to lose yet again.' He gave her a measured look. 'So—what do you plan to do now? Will you take advantage of Monsieur Newson's offer—if it still stands?'

'I'd rather burn the place to the ground.'

'The insurance company might find that suspicious,' he murmured.

'Probably—if we were insured,' Helen said shortly, and for the first time saw him look taken aback.

'You like to take risks,' he said.

'Sometimes I don't have a choice in the matter. I found my grandfather had let the premiums lapse.' She drank the rest of her tea and put down the mug. 'And now please leave. I've answered enough questions, and you have no further excuse to be here.'

'Except my own inclination,' he told her brusquely. 'And I ask again—what will you do next?'

'I shall open the house up for visitors, as I do every Saturday.' Her smile was swift and hard as she rose to her feet.

'I think no one would blame you if, for once, the house remained shut.'

'I'd blame myself,' she said. 'Because Monteagle needs every penny I can earn. And, anyway, I'd rather have something to do.' She paused. 'Please don't feel you have to take the tour again, or pay any more visits here,' she added pointedly. 'I'm sure you have places to go and people to see, so let's both of us get on with our lives. Shall we?'

But he ignored that. 'Is that truly how you see your future?' His brows lifted. 'Welcoming crowds of the curious and the bored *pour toujours*? Serving them tea?'

She met his gaze. 'Yes,' she said. 'If I have to. I told you— I'll do anything to save Monteagle.'

'Will you?' he asked softly. 'I wonder, *ma mie*. I very much wonder. For example, will you have dinner with me this evening?'

Her lips parted in sheer astonishment. She said unevenly, 'My God, you never give up, do you? Do you think I'm in any mood to listen to another of your insensitive—tasteless invitations? Can't you understand that I've just lost the man I love?'

'You are planning to starve to death as an act of revenge?' He had the gall to sound faintly amused.

'No,' Helen said stormily. 'But I'd rather die than have dinner with you.'

He was laughing openly now, to her fury. 'A fate worse than death, *ma belle*? I always thought that involved far more than simply sharing a meal.'

She marched to the door and held it open. 'Just get out of my house and don't come back.'

'Your house,' Marc said softly, unmoved and unmoving. 'And how much longer will you be able to call it that, unless you find financial support—and quickly? You said you would do anything to save Monteagle. So, can you afford to reject my offer of assistance unheard?'

There was silence in the room, broken only by the crackle of the burning wood and the swift flurry of her own ragged breathing.

She felt like a small animal, caught in the headlights of an approaching juggernaut. Only she'd been trapped, instead, by her own words, she realised bitterly.

She said thickly, 'What—kind of help?'

'We will not discuss that now. Your mood is hardly—receptive. Also,' he added silkily, 'you have work to do. We will speak again later.'

He walked past her and she shrank backwards, flattening herself against the thick wooden door as she remembered, only too well, his last leavetaking. The hardness of his body against hers. The touch—the taste of his mouth.

He favoured her with a brief, sardonic smile. *À tout à l'heure!'* he told her quietly, and then he was gone.

Did you take an order from the people in the far corner, Miss Helen?' asked Daisy, entering the kitchen with a stacked tray of dirty dishes. 'Because they're playing up at having to wait.'

Helen, lost in thought at the sink, started guiltily. 'Oh, Lord,' she muttered. 'I forgot all about them. I'll serve them next,' she added hurriedly, collecting one of the larger teapots from the shelf.

'Your mind's not on it today, and no wonder. You should have gone for a nice lie-down in your room,' Daisy said severely. 'I'd have got George to do the waiting on.'

'I'm fine,' Helen said untruthfully. 'And I really prefer to be busy,' she added placatingly.

Daisy sniffed. 'There's busy and busy,' she said. 'You've just put cream in the sugar basin.'

Swearing under her breath, Helen relaid the tray and carried it out into the sunshine.

Once again she'd been astonished at the number of visitors, but they hadn't been as easy to handle as last week's selection.

'You don't see much for your money,' one man had complained.

'We're hoping to extend the tour to other rooms in the house quite soon,' Helen had explained, but he'd glared at her.

'Well, that's no good to me,' he'd said. 'I've already paid.'

And a large family party had demanded why there were no games machines for kiddies, or even a playground, and why they couldn't play football in an adjoining field.

'Because my tenant wouldn't like it,' Helen had said, in a tone that brooked no further argument.

It had been an afternoon of moans and niggles, she thought wearily, and from the look of strained tolerance she'd glimpsed on Marion Lowell's face at one point, she wasn't the only sufferer.

Altogether, this was the day from hell, she thought. And she still couldn't decide what to do about Marc Delaroche and his dinner invitation.

Instinct told her to refuse. Reason suggested that if Monteagle's welfare was involved she should at least give him a hearing. But not over dinner, she thought. That was too much like a date rather than a business meeting.

'And about time.' Helen was greeted truculently by a red-haired woman as she reached the corner table and set down the heavy tray. She and her glum-looking husband peered suspiciously at the plates of scones and cakes. 'Is this all we get? Aren't there are any sandwiches? Ham would do. We've got a growing lad here.'

Growing outwards as well as upwards, Helen noticed with disfavour, as the child in question dug a podgy finger into the bowl of cream.

She said quietly, 'I'm sorry, it's a standard tea. But everything is home-made.'

The little boy glared at her. 'Aren't there any crisps? And where's my drink?'

'He doesn't like tea,' his mother explained in a tone that invited congratulation. 'He wants orange squash.'

Helen repressed a sigh. 'I'll see what I can do.'

Back in the kitchen, she halved oranges from the fruit bowl, squeezed out their juice, and put it in a glass with a pinch of sugar and some ice cubes.

Improvisation, she told herself with mild triumph as she took the drink outside.

'What's that?' The boy stabbed an accusing finger at it. 'I want a real drink. That's got bits in it.'

'They're bits of orange—' Helen began.

'Yuck.' The child's face twisted into a grimace. 'I'm not drinking that.' And he picked up the glass and threw the contents at Helen, spattering her with the sticky juice.

She gasped and fell back, wiping her face with her hand, then felt hands grip her shoulders, putting her to one side.

'Go and get clean,' Marc directed quietly. 'I will deal with this.'

She hadn't even been aware of his approach. She wanted to tell him she could manage, but she wasn't sure it was true.

She turned away, walking quickly back to the house, stripping off her ruined apron as she went, her colour rising as she became aware of sympathetic smiles and murmurs from other customers.

She looked back over her shoulder and saw Marc talking to the husband. Noticed the other man rise uncomfortably to his feet, his face sullen, gesturing to his family to follow.

When she reached the kitchen she found Lottie waiting, her face grave and troubled. 'Honey,' she said, 'I'm so sorry.'

Helen bit her lip. 'I see you've heard the news.' She ran cold water into a bowl and put her stained apron to soak.

Lottie nodded unhappily. 'It's all round the village. I still can't quite believe it.'

'It's perfectly true.' Helen lifted her chin. 'Nigel is being splendidly conventional and marrying his boss's daughter. I haven't worked out yet whether he ever meant to tell me to my face, or if he hoped I'd simply—fade away and save him the trouble.'

'Bastard,' said Lottie, with some force. 'But it certainly explains the special buffet episode.' She snorted. 'Well, I've rung his poisonous mother and told her to find another caterer.'

Helen smiled wanly. 'It's a lovely thought,' she said. 'But it's also the kind of gesture you can't afford any more than I could.' She glanced round her. 'Where's Daisy?'

'She said she had something to do upstairs and that she'd ask Mrs Lowell to collect the tea money. She probably thought we'd want to talk in private.'

'I don't think I have much privacy left,' Helen said ruefully. 'Not if the whole village knows.' She paused. 'I also found out this morning that I'd been turned down for that grant.'

'Oh, no,' Lottie groaned. 'That's really evil timing.' She gave Helen a compassionate look. 'Well—they say bad luck comes in threes, so let's hope your final misfortune is a minor one.'

Helen bit her lip as she refilled the kettle and set it to boil. 'No such luck, I'm afraid. It's happened—and it's another disaster.'

Lottie whistled. 'Tell me something—is there some gruesome family curse hanging over the Fraynes that you've never thought to mention?'

'If only.' Helen grinned faintly. 'Good business, a family curse. I'd have given it a whole page in the guidebook.'

Lottie started to laugh, and then, as if some switch had been operated, the amusement was wiped from her face, to be replaced by astonishment bordering on awe.

Helen turned quickly and saw Marc in the doorway, completely at his ease, arms folded across his chest and one shoulder propped nonchalantly against the frame.

He said, '*Je suis désolè*. I am intruding.'

'No,' Lottie denied with something of a gulp, getting quickly to her feet. 'No, of course not. I'm Charlotte Davis—Lottie— a friend of Helen's from the village.'

He sent her a pleasant smile. '*Enchanté, mademoiselle*. And I am Marc Delaroche—*à votre service*.'

To her eternal credit, Lottie didn't allow herself even a flicker of recognition.

Helen swallowed. 'What—what did you say to those people just now?' she asked a little breathlessly.

'I suggested only that they might prefer the Monteagle Arms. They accepted my advice.' He walked across to the table and put down some money. 'They also paid,' he added laconically. He paused. 'Tell me, *ma mie*, are many of your customers like that?'

'Not usually.' She went over to the stove and busied herself with the kettle. 'I'm just having a generally bad day, I think.' She hesitated. 'Would you like some coffee?' she offered unwillingly—as he instantly detected.

'*Merci.*' He slanted a faint grin at her. 'But I will leave you to talk in peace to your friend.' He added softly, 'I came only to say that I have reserved a table for eight o'clock at the Oxbow. I hope you will feel able to join me.'

He gave them both a slight bow and walked back into the sunshine, leaving a tingling silence behind him.

It was broken at last by Lottie. 'Wow,' she said reverently. 'Don't pretend even for a moment that he's your third disaster.'

'Oh, you're as bad as Mrs Lowell,' Helen said crossly, aware that her face had warmed. 'She was rhapsodising about him last week.'

'You mean this is his second visit?' Lottie's brows shot skywards. 'Better and better.' She eyed Helen. 'So, what are you going to wear tonight?'

'Nothing!'

Lottie grinned wickedly. 'Well, it would certainly save him time and effort,' she said. 'But a little obvious for a first date, don't you think?'

Helen's colour deepened hectically. 'I didn't mean that—as you well know,' she said, carrying the coffee back to the table. 'And it's not a date. In fact, I have no intention of having dinner with Monsieur Delaroche—tonight or any other time.'

'Nonsense,' Lottie said briskly. 'Of course you're going. Why not?'

Helen sank limply on to the nearest chair. 'You seem to have forgotten about Nigel.'

'Unfortunately, no,' said Lottie. 'But I'm working on it, and so should you.' She gave Helen's arm a quick squeeze. 'And what more could you ask than for a seriously attractive man to wine and dine you?'

'You really think that a meal at the Oxbow could console me in any way for Nigel?' Helen shook her head. 'Lottie—I'm really hurting. He's always been part of my life—and now he's gone.'

'Helen—be honest. You had a crush on him when you were thirteen and decided he was the man of your dreams. He went along with it for a while, but he's spent less and less time here for over a year now. Some love affair.'

'No,' Helen said, biting her lip. 'It never was. That's the trouble. I—I wanted to wait. So it wasn't an affair at all, in the real meaning of the word.'

'Oh,' said Lottie slowly. 'Well—that's one less thing to regret.'

'But I do regret it,' Helen told her miserably. She sighed. 'Oh, God, what a fool I've been. And I've lost him. So do you see now why I can't go out tonight? It would be unbearable.'

'Then stay here and brood,' Lottie told her robustly. 'And why not have "victim" tattooed across your forehead while you're about it?'

Helen gave her a bitter look. 'I didn't know you could be so heartless. How would you like to face people if you'd been dumped?'

'Darling, I'm trying to be practical.' Lottie drank some coffee. 'And I'd infinitely prefer to be out, apparently having a good time with another man, than nursing a broken heart on my own. Who knows? People might even think you dumped Nigel rather than the other way round. Think about it.' She paused. 'Anyway, why did you say it wasn't a date with Marc Delaroche?'

'Because it's more of a business meeting.' Helen still looked morose. 'He's got some plan for helping Monteagle now the grant's fallen through. Or he says he has.'

'All the more reason to go, then.'

'But I don't want to feel beholden to him,' Helen said passionately. 'I—I don't like him. And I don't know what you all see in him,' she added defiantly.

'Helen—' Lottie's tone was patient '—he's incredibly rich and fabulously sexy. You don't think that you're being a mite picky?'

Helen said in a low voice, 'It's not just that. I—I think I'm frightened of him.' Her laugh cracked in the middle. 'Isn't that ridiculous?'

Lottie's expression was very gentle. 'A little, maybe. But there's not much he can do in a crowded restaurant.' She frowned. 'I wonder how the hell he managed to get a table at the Oxbow, it being Saturday and all.'

Helen shrugged listlessly. 'He's someone who likes to have his own way. I don't suppose he gets many refusals.'

Lottie gave her a wry grin. 'Then meeting you might be good for his soul.' She paused, then added thoughtfully, 'Or he might even be good for yours.'

She picked up her beaker and rose. 'Now, let's have a quick scan through your wardrobe and see what might be suitable for the best restaurant in miles.'

This is still such a bad idea, Helen thought a few hours later as she looked at herself in the mirror.

The dress she was wearing was in a silky fabric the dark green of a rose leaf, and made in a wrap-around style, with a sash that passed twice round her slender waist and fastened at the side in a bow.

It made her skin look exotically pale, and her newly washed hair glint with gold and bronze lights.

Lottie had spotted it at once, of course. 'So, what's this?' she'd asked, taking it from the rail. 'Clearly never worn, because it's still got the price tag. How long have you had it?'

'Not that long.' Helen moved a shoulder restively, her voice slightly husky. 'I—I bought it for my engagement party.' She forced a smile. 'Counting my chickens again. Stupid of me, wasn't it?'

'Not at all.' Lottie's tone was comforting. 'And you can put it to good use tonight instead,' she added, spreading it across Helen's bed.

'No,' Helen said sharply. 'I got it for Nigel. I won't wear it for anyone else. I can't.'

'What will you do with it, then? Wrap it in lavender and shed tears over it, like a latter-day Miss Havisham?' Lottie gave her a swift hug. 'Babe, you can't waste the only decent thing you've got—especially when you need to make a good impression.'

'And why should I want to do that?' Helen lifted her chin.

'Monteagle, of course,' Lottie told her with a cat-like smile. 'Did you get shoes as well?'

'Green sandals.' Helen pointed reluctantly. 'They're in that box.'

'You'll have to paint your toenails too,' Lottie mused. 'I'd better pop home and get my manicure stuff, because I bet you haven't any. And you'll need a wrap. I'll lend you the pashmina Simon sent me. But don't spill vintage champagne all over it.'

The promised wrap was now waiting on the bed, together with the small kid bag that matched the sandals.

I was so sure, Helen thought, her throat muscles tightening. So secure in my dreams of the future. And so blind...

And now she had to work towards a totally different kind of future.

She'd had plenty of time to think after Lottie had completed her ministrations and departed.

Lying back in a scented bath, she'd reviewed her situation and come up with a plan. She could not afford to pay for the restoration of the entire house, of course, but perhaps Marc Delaroche might help her raise sufficient capital to refurbish the bedrooms at least, so that she and Daisy could offer bed and breakfast accommodation. Possibly with a few extra refinements.

Spend the night in the haunted bedroom! she'd thought, with self-derision. See the ghost of the first Helen Frayne, if not the second.

I could even rattle a few chains outside the door.

Joking apart, the scheme had a lot to recommend it, she told herself. It could supply her with just the regular income she needed.

And if she could prove herself, even in a small way, the conventional banking system might be more ready to back her.

But first she had to persuade Marc that it was a workable plan, and an alternative to whatever assistance he was prepared to give.

And therefore it was—just—worth making an effort with her appearance.

Only now the moment had come. Daisy had tapped on her door to say that he was waiting downstairs, causing all her concerns and doubts to come rushing back.

Because she was taking a hell of a risk. She'd said it herself—Marc Delaroche was a man who liked his own way—so what on earth made her think she could manipulate him into doing what she wanted?

Besides, she already knew he had his own agenda. *On my next visit I shall expect to spend the night.*

She'd tried to block that out of her mind—as with so much else that had passed between them.

But now the words were ringing loud and clear in her head, especially as she'd spent some considerable time getting herself dressed and beautified for him—like some harem girl being prepared for the Sultan's bed, she thought, and grimaced at the analogy.

Her skin was smooth and scented. Her eyes looked twice their normal size, shaded, with darkened lashes, and the colour of her dress had turned them from hazel to green. Her mouth glowed with soft coral, as did the tips of her hands and feet.

She picked up her wrap and bag, and went along the Gallery to the broad wooden staircase.

Marc was below her, in the entrance hall, pacing restlessly, but as he looked up at her he checked suddenly, his entire attention arrested and fixed on her, his eyes widening and his mouth suddenly taut.

She felt a strange shiver of awareness rake her body, and for a moment she wanted to turn and run—back to her room, to safety. Back to the girl she really was.

Because for the first time it occurred to her that she was not simply scared of Marc Delaroche.

I'm frightened of myself, she whispered silently. And of the stranger I've just become—for him.

She drew a deep shaking breath, then very slowly she walked down the stairs to meet him.

CHAPTER FIVE

THE restaurant was just as crowded as Lottie had predicted. Apart from their own, Helen could see only one vacant table, and that was reserved too.

She was conscious of a surprised stir as they entered, and knew that she'd been recognised by at least half the people in the room, and that the rumour mill had been functioning well. She tried to ignore the speculative looks and whispered comments as, with Marc's hand cupped under her elbow, she followed the head waiter across the room.

But a shock wave was preferable every time to a ripple of sympathy, she thought, straightening her shoulders. Lottie had been right about that too.

And it was difficult to feel too humiliated over Nigel when she'd been brought here in a chauffeur-driven car and was now being seated at a candlelit table in an alcove where a bottle of Dom Perignon on ice and two glasses were waiting for them.

And also when she was being accompanied by the most attractive man in the room, she acknowledged reluctantly.

Tonight, as she'd noticed in the car, he was freshly shaven, and the dark mane of hair had been combed into a semblance of order. Close-fitting dark pants set off his long legs, and his well-laundered white shirt was enhanced by a silk tie with the colour and richness of a ruby. The light tweed jacket, slung over his shoulder, shouted 'cashmere'.

Certainly there'd been no escaping the frank envy in some of the female eyes as they watched her progress.

Oh, God, she thought, swallowing, I must be unbelievably shallow to find all that even a minor comfort.

'It has a good reputation, this place,' her companion commented as the champagne was poured and the menus arrived.

'Yes,' Helen agreed, glad of a neutral topic. 'Lottie reckons

71

it's the best food in miles. And they do rooms as well,' she added, her mind returning to Monteagle and its problems.

'*C'est vrai?*' he queried softly. 'You wish me to reserve one for later, perhaps?'

Her head lifted from the menu she was studying as if she'd been shot, her mouth tightening indignantly as she saw the wicked amusement in the dark eyes.

She said between her teeth, 'Will you—please—not say things like that?'

'Forgive me,' he said, showing no obvious signs of repentance. 'But you are so easy to tease, *ma mie*, and you blush so adorably. Calm yourself with some champagne.'

'Is there something to celebrate?' She picked up her glass.

'Who knows?' He shrugged. 'But, anyway, let us drink to Monteagle—and its future.'

'Actually,' Helen began, 'I've been giving that some thought and—'

He lifted a silencing hand. 'Later, *cherie*,' he told her softly. 'You must learn how the game is played. And also accept that a man rarely grants favours on an empty stomach,' he added drily.

'But it's not a game,' she protested. 'Not to me.'

'*Quand même,*' he said. 'We will eat first.'

His rules, Helen thought resentfully, transferring her attention back to the list of food. A man who likes his own way. And just how far is he prepared to go in order to achieve it? she wondered, and shivered slightly.

But in the meantime she might as well enjoy the food, as this would probably be her first and last visit. She chose potted shrimps for her first course, following them with a rack of lamb, roasted pink, with grilled vegetables.

Marc ordered *tournedos* of beef, with *foie gras* and dark-gilled mushrooms, served with a Madeira sauce.

The Burgundy he picked to accompany the meal seemed to caress her throat like velvet.

'Will you tell me something?' Helen said, once they'd been served and the waiters had departed.

'If I can.'

'Why did the committee bother to hear me if they meant to turn me down?'

'We interview every applicant, or those that represent them. Mainly we concentrate on projects that will revive the tourist industry in former trouble spots, or attract it to areas entirely off the beaten track.' He shrugged. 'Your application was thought to be interesting, but not particularly deserving. Unluckily for you, *cherie*, you do not have to walk ten miles to find water each day, and your home is lit by the flick of a switch,' he added drily.

'Only,' she said, 'if I can afford to pay the bill.'

They ate in silence for a moment or two, and she was just nerving herself to mention the bed and breakfast idea when he said, 'Hélène—in an ideal world, what would you wish for Monteagle?'

'That's simple. I'd like it to be my home again, but with the money to maintain it properly, of course.' She sighed. 'No tour parties, no cream teas. Just peace, comfort and privacy. The way it once was. And the way a home should be, don't you think?'

'I would not know,' he told her drily. 'I have an apartment in Paris and a hotel suite in London. When I was a child my father never settled in any place for very long,' he added with a faint shrug. 'Only when he retired did he find somewhere— a vineyard in Burgundy with a small dilapidated château, close to the village where he was born. He planned to live there and make wine, but he died very suddenly before it was even habitable.'

'What happened to it?' she asked.

'I sold it to an English family in search of *la vie douce*.' He smiled faintly. 'Only God knows if they ever found it.'

'You weren't tempted to live there yourself?'

'And tend my vines in the sun?' He shook his head. 'I have factories to produce, and a world to travel in order to sell them.'

As he spoke he looked past her, and Helen saw him stiffen slightly, the dark brows snapping together. 'Ah,' he said softly. '*C'est complet*. The last table is now occupied—and by people you know, *ma belle*.'

She said, bewildered, 'People…?' And then stopped, staring at him, appalled.

'Oh, God,' she said unevenly. 'It's Nigel, isn't it? And his new lady?'

'And an older couple—*ses parents, sans doute*,' Marc drawled. Then, as Helen began to push her plate away, he reached across the table and captured her hands in his, holding them firmly. '*Doucement, cherie,*' he ordered softly. 'You are going nowhere.'

'But I must,' she whispered frantically. 'I can't stay here and see them together. I can't…'

'But you do not have to,' he said. 'It is all quite simple. You just look at me instead.' He lifted her hands to his lips, brushing light kisses across her white knuckles, nibbling gently at the tips of her trembling fingers, while she sat as if mesmerised allowing it to happen.

His eyes smiled into hers. 'Think, Hélène,' he urged quietly. 'If you run away, then they will know they have the power to make you suffer—and so they win. Better that you remain here—with me—and we finish our meal, *hein*?'

He released her hands and refilled her glass, wincing slightly as she took an unguarded panicky gulp of the precious wine.

She said huskily, 'Have they seen me?'

'I notice a certain *chagrin*, yes.' His mouth twisted. '*La mère*, I think, wishes to go, but her husband—*c'est un homme inflexible*, and he will get his way.'

'And Nigel?' She swallowed. 'How—how does he look?'

He shrugged. 'He seems to have survived his wetting in the lake.'

'Oh, God,' she said miserably. 'He'll never forgive me for that.'

'Perhaps,' he said. 'But that can no longer be allowed to matter to you.' He paused to let that sink in, then nodded at her plate. 'Now eat, *ma mie*, and take your time. After all, we still have the dessert to come. The apricot soufflés, I think, which have to be cooked to order, and will prove, therefore, that we are in no particular hurry.'

He cut off a sliver of beef and proffered it to her on his fork. 'In the meantime, try this, and—smile at me a little.'

'It's all right for you.' Unwillingly she did as she was told. The fact that he was talking sense made his advice no more palatable. 'You're not the one whose heart is being broken.'

He gave her a sardonic look. 'And nor are you, *cherie*, although you may not believe it at this moment.'

'How can you say that? How can someone like you possibly understand?' Helen asked passionately.

His brows lifted. 'You speak as if I was something less than human. Yet, *je t'assure*, I share all the normal emotions.' He smiled at her coolly. 'You wish me to demonstrate?'

'*No!*' Her face warmed. 'I meant that you've obviously never loved someone all your life as I've loved Nigel.' She shook her head. 'Why, I've never even looked at another man.'

'Perhaps because you have never had the chance to do so,' he said, unmoved. 'And your life is far from over. Now, eat something, *ma belle*, before your lack of appetite is noticed.'

Helen shot him a mutinous look from under her lashes, then reluctantly complied.

As they ate, Marc chatted to her lightly, asking mainly questions about the history of Monteagle, encouraging her to expand her monosyllabic replies into real animation as she warmed to her subject.

Making it almost possible, she realised with a sense of shock, for her to believe that she was there with him because she wished it, and not as a matter of expedience.

But she had to convince him of her enthusiasm, and her will to work, she thought, if she was to persuade him to lend her the money for the guest house scheme.

If only Nigel hadn't been there she'd have been able to outline her plan by now—have a proper business discussion, she thought with vexation. As it was, her companion had taken advantage of the delay while they waited for the soufflés, and taken her hand again, and was now playing gently with her fingers.

She glanced up, a muted protest already forming on her lips, but as their eyes met, and she saw the frank desire that smoked his gaze, she forgot completely what she was going to say.

She looked away swiftly, hating the involuntary colour that warmed her cheeks, trying unavailingly to release her hand from the caress of his long fingers.

She said haltingly, 'I—I don't know how you can—pretend like this.'

His faint smile was crooked. 'But I am not pretending, *cherie*,' he told her quietly. 'I want you. I have made no secret of it.'

She stared down at the tablecloth. 'Then you're due for a serious disappointment, Monsieur Delaroche. Even if I was in the market for an affair—which I'm not—you'd be the last person on earth I'd choose.'

'Then at least we agree on something,' Marc drawled. 'Because I do not want an *affaire* either. *Au contraire*, I wish you to become my wife.'

Helen was very still suddenly. She could feel her throat muscles tightening in shock. The blood drumming crazily in her ears.

'If—this is some kind of joke,' she managed hoarsely, 'then it's in very poor taste.'

'There is no joke,' he said. 'I am asking you to marry me, *ma belle*, and I am completely serious.'

She said, 'But you don't know anything about me. We've met three times at most.' She shook her head. 'We're strangers, for heaven's sake. You must be mad even to think of such a thing.'

'I do not suggest that the ceremony should take place next week.' He smiled at her. 'I intend to court you, Hélène. Give you some time to accustom yourself to the idea.' He paused. 'To all kinds of ideas,' he added drily.

He meant sleeping with him, she realised dazedly. She would have to face the prospect of him making love to her. With a sense of shock she found herself remembering their last encounter—the hard strength of his arms and the relentless heated urgency of his mouth on hers. Even though they'd both been fully dressed, she'd still been aware of every inch of his lean body against hers. And the thought of being held—touched—without the barrier of clothing, sent her mouth dry with panic.

He wanted her. He'd said so. Therefore he would not expect to be fended off—kept waiting until after the wedding.

Except there would be no wedding, she told herself with sudden fierceness. So why was she treating his outrageous proposal as if it was all cut and dried?

She said, 'You're wasting your time, *monsieur*. Did you think I'd be so terrified of being a spinster that you could catch me on the rebound?' She shook her head. 'You're wrong. Nothing on earth could persuade me to marry you.'

'Not even Monteagle?' he challenged. 'You wish it to become a home again. You said so.' He shrugged. '*Moi aussi*. Become my wife, and I will make funds available for the whole house to be restored in the way that you want.'

'No,' she said huskily. 'That's impossible. I couldn't—I can't.'

'Yet you said at the interview that you would do anything to save it.' He sat back in his chair, watching her from under half-closed lids. 'Clearly your devotion to your house is not as profound as you claim.'

'When I said that I was desperate.' Helen lifted her chin. 'But now I have a plan.'

'*D'accord,*' he said. 'A plan that you wish to share with me. But after we have finished our desserts,' he added calmly, apparently unfazed by her refusal, just as a waiter bore down on them with the soufflés, tall as chefs' hats, in their porcelain dishes.

She said unsteadily, 'You think I could eat anything else—after that bombshell?'

'*Mais, j'insiste.* One spoonful at least. To calm you,' he added, his mouth twisting wryly.

Unwilling, totally unnerved, she obeyed. The delicate flavour and texture melted deliciously on her tongue, and was impossible, she discovered, to resist.

So,' Marc said at last, putting down his spoon, 'what is this plan, and how will it save Monteagle?'

Helen took a breath. 'I want to restore and refurbish all the bedrooms so that I can offer bed and breakfast to tourists,' she said baldly.

His face gave nothing away. 'And you have costed this scheme? You have taken into your calculations the price of supplying each room with a bathroom *en suite*? Also refurbishing the dining room so that your guests have somewhere to eat this *petit dejeuner* without the ceiling falling on their heads? And, of course, there will be the updating of the kitchen to be considered, so that it meets the demands of Health and Safety regulations.'

'Well, no,' Helen admitted, disconcerted. 'Not entirely. Because I've only just thought of it. But I'll get proper estimates for all the work for you to approve first.'

'For me?' he queried, brows lifted. 'How does this concern me?'

She bit her lip, suddenly wishing that her earlier rejection of his proposal had been a little less forceful. 'I was hoping that— you would lend me the money.'

There was a silence. 'Ah,' he said. 'But you have forgotten that there is an offer already on the table, where I give you all the money you need and you become my wife.'

She said breathlessly, 'But if you gave me a loan we wouldn't need to be married. And I'd have thought you were the last man on earth in the market for a wife.'

The dark eyes glinted at her. 'It does not occur to you, *ma mie*, that, much like yourself, I might be deeply and irresistibly in love?'

Helen felt as if all the breath had suddenly been choked out of her lungs. She stared at him, her eyes widening endlessly.

She said in a small, cracked voice, 'I don't—understand...'

'No? But you have only yourself to blame, *ma chère*. If you had not written and spoken about Monteagle with such passion, then I would not have been tempted to come and see it for myself. *Et voilà*. The rest, as they say, is history.'

She clutched at her reeling senses. She said huskily, 'You— mean that what you really want—is Monteagle. *Monteagle?* That's what you're saying?' She shook her head. 'Oh, I don't believe it. It's impossible, besides being ridiculous—ludicrous. You *can't*...'

His brows lifted. '*Pourquoi pas?* Why not? Along with my lack of humanity, do you also claim that I have no feeling for history—or appreciation of beauty?'

'How do I know,' she said stormily, 'what you think—what you feel about anything? You're a complete stranger, and as far as I'm concerned you always will be.' She looked at him, her eyes flashing. 'But you're talking about *my home*. Mine.'

'At the moment, yes.' He shrugged. 'But for how much longer without serious investment? You say you will not consider the offer of Monsieur Newson, so I offer an alternative. One of its advantages is that you will be able to go on living in the house you prize so highly.'

'Except,' she said, quietly and clearly, 'I'd be obliged to live with you.'

'It's an uncertain world, *cherie*,' he said mockingly. 'And I travel to dangerous places. Think of this—I could be dead within the year, and you would be a wealthy widow.' He added sardonically, 'I might even die on our wedding night—of ecstasy.'

He saw her flinch, and laughed softly.

Helen sat in silence, her teeth doing yet more damage to her ill-used lower lip, as a waiter arrived with a pot of coffee and a bottle of cognac.

When they were once again alone, she said, 'Please reconsider lending me the money. I swear I'll work night and day, and repay you in full.'

'Yes, *ma belle*, you will,' he said softly. 'But in coin of my choosing.' He paused to allow her to absorb that. 'And my offer remains a gift, not a loan.' He smiled at her. 'A wedding present, perhaps, from the groom to his bride.'

Helen stared down at her hands, clenched painfully in her lap. 'Why are you doing this?' she asked in a low voice. 'You're forcing me to sell myself to you for Monteagle. What kind of man does something like that?'

'A rich one.' He sounded appallingly casual—even amused. 'If something I want is for sale, *cherie*, then I buy it.'

'No matter what the consequences?'

He shrugged. 'For me, they are good. I am gaining a house I want and a woman I desire. And maybe I have reached a time in my life when a home and children have become important to me.'

Her lips parted in a gasp. 'You think for one minute—you really expect me to have your baby?'

'Another consequence of marriage,' Marc drawled unsmilingly. 'If you still believe in the stork, *ma mie*, you have been misinformed.' He paused. 'But I am forcing you to do nothing, Hélène. Understand that. I merely offer you a solution to your most pressing problem. It is for you to decide whether you accept my proposal or deny me.'

He gave her a measuring look. 'And you have twenty-four hours in which to make up your mind,' he added coolly.

She picked up her glass and took a mouthful of cognac, feeling it crackle in her throat. At the same time she was conscious of a faint dizziness. It might be caused by the shocks of the past hour, but could also be ascribed to the amount of alcohol she'd unwittingly taken on board, she realised.

Well, there would be no more of that, at least. She wasn't accustomed to it, and she needed to keep her wits about her now as never before, she thought grimly.

She looked back at him defiantly. 'Is this how you usually propose marriage—by ultimatum?'

The hardness of his mouth relaxed into a swift, unexpected grin. 'Until this moment, *cherie*, I have never proposed marriage at all. Other things, yes,' he added shamelessly. 'But not marriage.'

She gave him a fulminating look. 'I suppose I should feel flattered,' she said icily. 'But I don't.' She reached for her bag. 'May we go now, please?'

He was still amused. '*D'accord.*' He signalled for the bill while Helen braced herself for the walk to the door, which would involve passing Nigel and his new fiancée.

But when she turned to leave she saw only an empty table, in the process of being cleared by the staff, and checked in surprise.

'They left about ten minutes ago,' Marc informed her quietly. 'They did not seem to be enjoying their evening.' He paused. 'Or perhaps your Nigel feared another dousing—from an ice bucket.'

Helen ignored that. 'Will you ask Reception to get me a taxi, please?' she requested with dignity.

She realised uneasily that she was having to choose her words, and her steps, with care, so the sooner she was rid of her companion, the better.

His brows lifted. 'My car and driver will be waiting,' he pointed out.

'But I really need to be alone,' she said. 'Surely even you can understand that?'

'"Even you,"' he repeated pensively. 'I see I shall have to change your low opinion of me, *cherie*.'

'By forcing me into marriage?' She shook her head. 'I don't think so.' She paused, lifting her chin. 'And now I'd really like to go home.'

He said lightly, 'As you wish,' and went to the reception desk.

'Your cab will be ten minutes,' he told her on his return. 'Shall I wait with you until it arrives?'

'No,' Helen said hastily, then added a belated, 'Thank you.' She'd half expected a protest, but all he said was a casual, '*A bientôt,*' and went.

There was no avoiding the fact that she would be seeing him again—and soon, she thought wearily. After all, he'd given her only twenty-four hours in which to make up her mind—or rack her brains for a way out.

She still felt faintly giddy, so she made her way over to a high-backed chair in the shelter of an enormous parlour palm and sat down, leaning back and closing her eyes.

When she heard the main door open she assumed her cab had arrived early, but instead she heard Nigel's voice peremptorily addressing the receptionist.

'My mother seems to have mislaid her scarf. Could someone look in the cloakroom for me? See if it's there?'

Helen, transfixed, had a fleeting impulse to climb into the palm and vanish.

But it was too late. Nigel had seen her and was crossing the foyer. She got to her feet, her fingers tightening defensively round the strap of her bag.

'All alone?' he asked unpleasantly. 'Dumped you already, has he?'

She flushed. 'No, he hasn't,' she said, adding recklessly, 'On the contrary, I'll be seeing him again tomorrow.'

'Well, you're certainly full of surprises, Helen. I'll grant you that.' He scanned her insolently from head to foot. 'You do know who you're dealing with, I suppose?'

'Yes,' she said. 'I know.'

'So, what the hell's a high-flyer like him doing in this backwater?' Nigel demanded.

She shrugged. 'Perhaps you should ask him that yourself.'

'Oh, I don't know him that well,' he said. 'It's Amanda. She's met him at parties in London and she could hardly believe her eyes when she saw you together. You're hardly his usual kind of totty.'

Helen steadied her voice. 'I'm sorry if she's disappointed.'

'She's not interested one way or the other,' Nigel said rather stiffly. 'He's certainly not her type. Nor does he believe in long-term relationships,' he added waspishly. 'Just in case you were hoping. Apparently he has a very low boredom threshold where women are concerned. Two months is the top limit for his involvements. None of his girls are kept around for longer. He's notorious for it.' He grinned nastily. 'And you haven't even lasted the night, sweetie.' He paused. 'So how *did* you meet him—as a matter of interest?'

'I can't imagine why it should be any of your concern,' she said, 'but he happened to be on the committee that turned me down the other day and he was curious about the house. It's as simple as that.'

Oh, God, she thought with a pang. *If only it were…*

'Oh, the *house*,' he said disparagingly. 'That explains it.'

'Thank you.' Helen said coldly, wishing desperately that her cab would arrive—or that she would be abducted by aliens.

He flushed slightly. 'Believe it or not, I'm trying to warn you for your own good. Although why I should bother after the trick you played on me this morning, God only knows,' he added sulkily. 'Do you know how long it took me to come up with an excuse for being soaked to the skin?'

'Am I supposed to care?' Helen threw back at him.

He shrugged, giving her a faintly injured look. 'We've known each other for a long time. I assumed it might be possible to remain friends.'

'Difficult,' she said, 'when we don't even occupy the same planet. And here's my taxi.' She offered him a small polite smile. 'Goodbye, Nigel, and—good luck.'

'And you,' he said venomously, 'deserve everything that's coming to you. When your house has gone, and your French millionaire has used you up and spat you out, don't come to me for a handout.'

There wasn't even a fountain to push him into this time, Helen thought, let alone the preferred swamp. And that was her sole regret as she walked away from him and out into the night.

Nor was it because of this brief confrontation that she found herself trembling as she sat huddled in the back of the taxi taking her home through the darkness.

It was Marc Delaroche who occupied her mind, imprinting himself indelibly on her inner vision.

My first real proposal of marriage, she thought, fighting back the bubble of hysteria rising within her. And it's from him.

She looked down at the hand he'd caressed and found she was clenching it into a fist.

As they headed through the village towards Monteagle her driver slowed as a car approached them, travelling smoothly and swiftly in the opposite direction.

Helen recognised it instantly. Oh, God, she thought, as she shrank further into her corner. *His car.* On its way back to the Monteagle Arms, no doubt.

But where on earth could he have been up till then? she asked herself in bewilderment. He should have returned long before her. Had his chauffeur become lost in the twisting lanes?

Whatever, he was far too close for her comfort. But perfectly poised for tomorrow, just an hour or so away, when he would come for his answer.

His package deal, she thought bitterly, for which he was apparently offering a blank cheque. Her house and herself—not necessarily in that order—and no expense spared. Or so he wanted her to believe...

It was—almost flattering. But she wasn't fooled, Helen told herself with sudden, desperate decision. It wasn't a genuine offer—not in a civilised society. It couldn't be...

He was merely testing her resolve, and of course he expected her to refuse. He probably relied on it.

After all, why should he want to spend a fortune on a place he'd seen briefly a couple of times?

And, besides, even a marriage that was only a business arrangement had too permanent a sound for someone who counted his relationships in days rather than years.

It's a wind-up, she thought with an inward sigh of relief, as the cab turned into Monteagle's gates. It has to be, and unfortunately I fell for it. Let him see I was rattled. Big mistake.

But at least she had a whole day to decide how to deal with it.

She considered, and immediately discarded, the idea of trying to rattle him in turn. Of letting him think she was actually tempted by his proposition and allowing him to talk her out of it. It might be amusing, but it was also dangerous.

He was too unpredictable, and—which annoyed her even more—invariably several steps ahead of her.

The sensible plan would be to tell him unsmilingly that the joke was over and request him to leave her in peace—seriously and permanently.

Except that might not be as simple as it sounded. Marriage might not be in the equation, but Marc Delaroche still wanted her. Inexperienced as she was, Helen was unable to deny that. If she was honest, she'd recognised it from their first encounter, with a stark female instinct she'd never known she possessed until that moment. And he was determined for his desire to be satisfied, however fleetingly.

It was that knowledge which dried her mouth and set up that deep inner trembling when he was near, invaded her thoughts when he was far away.

Nigel had never looked at her with such hungry intensity, she admitted painfully. Had never touched her skin as if he was caressing the petals of a flower. Had never stirred her senses to the edge of fear.

That alone should have warned her, she thought, as she paid off the driver and turned to go into the house.

There was no sign of Daisy, but the kitchen was filled with the aroma of coffee and the percolator bubbled away cheerfully.

She still felt fuzzy round the edges. Daisy's rich brew would clear her head and hopefully remove the shakiness in her legs too. Because she needed to be in total control, able to think positively. To plan tomorrow's response to Marc. Convince him once and for all, and with some force, that both she and Monteagle would remain forever beyond his reach.

She locked the back door, then took a mug from the big dresser and carried it, with the percolator, along to the library. She had some heavy decisions to make, so why not in comfort?

The lamps were lit, and a small fire was burning briskly in the hearth. God bless Daisy, she thought gratefully, and took one step forward into the room, only to halt in startled disbelief as she realised suddenly that she was not alone.

As she saw, with stomach-lurching shock, who was rising from the sofa to greet her.

'So, you are here at last,' Marc said softly. And his smile touched her in cool possession.

CHAPTER SIX

HER heart was beating like a stone being thrown against a wall. She stared back at him, her eyes widening endlessly in dismay. His jacket and tie had been discarded, tossed over the arm of the sofa, and his shirt was unbuttoned almost to the waist, the sleeves rolled back over his forearms.

He could not, she thought numbly, have announced his intentions any more clearly.

Her voice, when she finally found it, was hoarse. 'We—we said goodnight earlier. I saw your car on the way to the village—the hotel. So, what are you doing here?'

'You have a short memory, *ma belle*. It was my unfortunate chauffeur you saw going to the hotel.' The dark eyes glinted at her. 'I told you that on my next visit I intended to spend the night here in this house.'

'Yes, but I never thought...' She stopped, biting her lip, struggling for dignity. For some kind of rationality. Most of all, for some way of keeping him at arm's length—or an even greater distance. 'I prefer my guests to wait for an invitation.'

'I feared I might be made to wait for ever.' His mouth curled sardonically. He walked across and took the percolator from her wavering hand. 'Before you damage yourself, Hélène,' he added drily. 'Or me. Now, come and sit down.'

If she turned and ran he would only follow her, she knew, and she didn't want to demonstrate that kind of weakness—let him see that she was scared in any way.

So she moved on legs that did not seem to belong to her to the sofa, and sank down, grateful for its sagging support. A small table had been drawn up, holding a tray with cups, a cream jug and sugar bowl, plus a decanter of brandy and two glasses.

She said shakily, 'You certainly believe in making yourself at home—in every way.'

He shrugged. 'Perhaps because I believe that very soon this will be my home.' He sat down at the other end of the sofa and began to pour out the coffee.

She gave him a swift, wary glance. 'Isn't that a premature assumption?' She tried to keep her voice toneless. 'After all, you said you'd give me twenty-four hours to answer you.' She paused. 'And I also thought you'd have the decency to allow me to consider your proposition in private,' she added, with a touch of hauteur.

'But I decided I would pay court to you instead, *cherie*,' he drawled. 'Decency has always seemed to me such a dull virtue.'

His words, and the amused glance which accompanied them, were like an icy finger on her spine. Her hands were clamped round each other in an attempt to conceal the fact that they were trembling.

But she lifted her chin. 'Virtue?' she echoed cuttingly. 'I'm surprised you even know what the word means.'

'What a low opinion you have of me, *ma chère*,' Marc drawled, pouring measures of brandy into the glasses. 'But at least it releases me from any obligation to behave well.'

He leaned towards her and Helen flinched instinctively, realising too late that he was simply putting her coffee and brandy within her reach on the table. She saw his mouth tighten with sudden harshness, but when he spoke his voice was casual.

'And I made you a proposal, not a proposition. Perhaps you would like me to demonstrate the difference?'

'No,' Helen said too hastily. 'I wouldn't.'

'To hear you,' he said softly, 'one would think that your namesake in the portrait had been a Vestal Virgin and that you were following her example.' His gaze rested fleetingly on her mouth. 'Yet all the evidence denies this.'

'I dislike being railroaded,' Helen told him, flushing. She was searingly aware of the lean body lounging so casually beside her—and alarmed by her awareness. 'That does not, however, make me a prig.'

'I am glad of the assurance.' His tone was faintly mocking. 'So,' he went on after a pause, 'what did Nigel say to you that has put you so much on edge?'

Avoiding his gaze, she picked up her glass and drank some brandy. 'I don't know what you mean.'

'But you don't deny that there was another *rencontre*, I hope.' He spoke pleasantly enough, but she was aware of a faint, harsh edge in his voice. 'You are not the only one to take note of passing traffic, *ma mie*. I saw his car returning to the restaurant. You must still have been there. Also,' he added judiciously, 'you are paler than before, and your eyes look bruised. Was he angry, perhaps, at your attempt to drown him?'

Helen took another restorative gulp of brandy. 'It was mentioned,' she said shortly. 'But he seemed more interested in bad-mouthing you.'

His brows lifted. 'I was not aware I had the pleasure of his acquaintance.'

'But you know—his new lady.' She had to struggle to say the words. 'Apparently you've met—at parties in London.'

'Ah,' Marc said softly. 'But I meet a great many people at a great many parties, *cherie*. She made no particular impression on me at the time.'

'Well, she remembers you very well,' she said, adding recklessly, 'And your reputation.'

He laughed. 'Do I have one? I was not aware.'

'You're said to be anti-commitment.' Helen stared down into her glass. 'You never continue any of your love affairs longer than two months.' She paused. 'Can you deny it?'

'*Certainement.*' He was still amused. 'I can assure you, *ma mie*, that love has never entered into any of my *affaires*.'

She bit her lip. 'Now you're playing with words. But then you like to do that, don't you, Mr Delaroche? Proposal versus proposition, for example. Not that it matters,' she added, 'because we both know that it's just some private game for your own amusement, and that you haven't the slightest intention of getting married to me—or to anyone.'

She drew a breath. 'So, can it stop right now, please? I'm getting bored with the joke.'

He reached for his jacket, extracted something from the pocket, and put it on the table. Helen saw it was a jeweller's velvet covered box, and nearly choked on the brandy she was swallowing.

'This is not the moment I would have chosen,' he said quietly. 'But perhaps this will finally convince you that I have indeed asked you to be my wife. And that I am quite serious.'

The diamonds in the ring were a circle of fire surrounding the deeper flame of an exquisite ruby. Helen's lips parted in a silent gasp that was part wonder, part horror.

'So, do you believe at last?' His smile was grim. 'Now all you need do, *ma belle*, is make your decision.'

She said huskily, 'You—make it sound so easy.'

'Yes, or no,' he said. 'What could be simpler?'

She shook back her hair in a defiant gesture. 'You seem to forget that I'm being asked to choose between freedom and a life sentence—with a stranger.'

'And what does this freedom allow you, *ma mie*?' His voice was hard. 'The right to struggle, to work endlessly while the house you adore crumbles around you? Never to be able to indulge your beauty—your joy in life?'

He paused. 'Besides,' he added cynically. 'If your informants are correct, the maximum term for you to serve would be only two months. Is that really such a hardship?'

Helen stared at him, aware of a strange icy feeling in the pit of her stomach. Yes, she realised, with sudden paralysing shock. Yes, it would be—if, somehow, I started to care. If, however incredible it may seem, you taught me to want you—to love you—and then you walked away.

Because that would be more than hardship. It would be agony. And it could break my heart for ever...

She said in a small taut voice, 'I suspect, *monsieur*, that even one month of your intimate company might be more than I could bear.' She took a steadying breath. 'Is there really nothing else you would agree to—for Monteagle?'

'You are brutally frank.' His mouth twisted. 'So let me be the same. My answer to that is nothing. I take the house and you with it, Hélène. Or you will be left to your—freedom. The choice is yours.'

Her fingers played with a fold of her dress. 'I—I'll give you an answer tomorrow.'

He glanced at his watch. 'It is already tomorrow. You are running out of time, *ma belle.*'

She said with sudden heat, 'I wish—I really wish you'd stop saying that. Stop pretending that I'm beautiful.'

He studied her for a moment with half-closed eyes. 'Why do you do this?' he asked quietly eventually. 'Why do you so undervalue yourself?'

'Because I'm a realist.' She finished the brandy in her glass. 'I loved Nigel and he chose someone else. Someone beautiful.' She paused. 'I didn't get a chance to look at her at the restaurant, so I assume she is—beautiful.' Her glance challenged him. 'You're supposed to be a connoisseur, Monsieur Delaroche. What do you think—now that you've seen her again?'

He was silent for a moment, then he shrugged. 'She has her charms. Dark hair, a sexy mouth and a good body. And a tigress in bed, I imagine,' he added sardonically. 'Is that what you wanted to hear?'

Colour flared in her face, and her own completely unsexy mouth didn't seem to be working properly.

She said thickly, 'That's rather—too much information.'

'You hoped I would say she was plain and undesirable and that her only attraction is her father's money?' He spoke more gently. 'I wish it was so.'

'Don't pity me,' she said raggedly. 'Just don't—bloody pity me.'

He watched her for a moment, his expression wry. 'I think, Hélène, that you have had enough brandy.'

'Well, I don't agree.' She held out her glass defiantly. 'In fact I'd like some more—lots more—if you don't mind.'

Marc lifted the decanter. 'As you wish. But it is really too good to be used as an anaesthetic, *ma mie.*'

Helen tilted her chin. 'Maybe I want to be…' She tried the word 'anaesthetised' under her breath, but decided not to risk it. The room seemed very warm suddenly, and her head was swimming. 'Drunk,' seemed a safer alternative, and she said it twice just to make sure.

'I think you will achieve your ambition,' he told her drily. 'And sooner than you believe.'

She hoisted the refilled glass in his direction, aware that he seemed to have receded to some remote distance. Which was all to the good, of course. Perhaps, in time, if she went on drinking, he might disappear altogether.

'Cheers, *monsieur*,' she articulated with great care, and giggled at her success. Fine, she told herself defiantly, swallowing some more brandy. I'm—perfectly fine.

'*Salut, petite.*' His voice sounded very close. She felt the glass being removed from her hand, gently but firmly. Felt herself drawn nearer so that she was leaning against him, her cheek against his shoulder.

She knew she should resist, and swiftly, but her senses were filled with the warm male scent of him, and she was breathing the musky fragrance of the cologne he used. An odd weakness seemed to have invaded her body, and she wasn't sure she could get to her feet even if she tried, or stand upright if she did.

She was suddenly aware, too, that his hand was stroking her hair, softly, rhythmically, and she was shocked by this unexpected tenderness from Marc of all men. Because it seemed as if he had, in some strange way, become her sole rock in an ocean of desolation.

But that, she knew, was impossible. The complete opposite of the truth. Because he was danger, not comfort. Her enemy, not her friend. The predator, with herself as prey.

She moved suddenly, restlessly, trying to free herself, but the arm that held her was too strong, and the caressing hand almost hypnotic as it moved down to smooth the taut nape of her neck and the curve of her shoulder.

'*Sois tranquille.*' His voice was gentle. 'Be still, Hélène, and close your eyes. There is nothing to fear, I swear it.'

And somehow it was much simpler—almost imperative, in fact—to believe him and obey. To allow herself to drift endlessly as her weighted eyelids descended. And to surrender her own body's rhythms to the strong, insistent beat of his heart against hers.

She was never sure what woke her, but suddenly she was back to total consciousness, in spite of her aching head and her eyes, which some unfeeling person had filled with sand.

She took a cautious look round, then froze, all self-inflicted wounds forgotten. She was still on the sofa, but stretched out full-length in the arms of Marc, who was lying asleep beside her, his cheek resting on her hair.

She was so close to him, she realised, alarmed, that she could feel the warmth of his bare, hair-roughened chest through the thin fabric of her dress.

One arm was round her shoulders and the other lay across her body, his hand curving round her hipbone, and her movement was further restricted by the weight of his long leg, which was lying slightly bent over both of hers, imprisoning her in an intimacy as disturbing as it was casual.

Dear God, she moaned silently. How did I let this happen?

Her only small comfort was that apart from their shoes, which were on the floor, they were both dressed. But she could hardly have felt more humiliated if she'd woken up naked.

And just how long had this been going on anyway? she wondered miserably.

The lamp was still burning, but the fire was a pile of grey ash covering just one or two glowing embers.

Moving her arm carefully, she glanced at her watch and saw that it was nearly four a.m.

She took a steadying breath. I have to get out of here, she thought. Right now.

It didn't appear as if anything untoward had happened—in fact, she knew it hadn't—but she felt totally vulnerable like this, in his embrace. She certainly couldn't risk his waking and finding her there with him, in case he decided, after all, to—take advantage of the situation.

With the utmost caution she pushed his leg away, then slid,

inch by wary inch, from beneath his arm, putting down a hand to balance herself before lowering herself slowly to the floor.

She sat motionless for a moment, listening intently, but he did not stir and there was no change in his even breathing.

In spite of the pounding in her head, she managed to get to her feet. Then, sandals in hand, she tiptoed to the door and let herself out into the dark house. She knew every step of the way, every creaking floorboard to avoid as she fled to her bedroom. Once safely inside, out of breath and feeling slightly sick, she turned the key in the lock, and for good measure pushed a small wooden chair under the handle.

Then she stripped, letting her clothes lie where they fell, and crept into bed, pulling the covers over her head.

All that damned brandy. She groaned, fighting her nausea and praying for the bed to keep still. *I must have been insane. Why, anything could have happened while I was unconscious.*

Only to her own bewilderment it was apparent that nothing had. Instead, Marc had let her sleep, peacefully and comfortably.

So he can't have wanted me that much, after all, she thought, turning over and burying her face in the pillow. *It's the house—just the house.* And found herself wondering why that particular realisation should sting so much?

She certainly didn't need to be desired by a serial womaniser, she reminded herself forcefully.

She had to think, clearly and rationally, she told herself. Find a watertight reason for turning him down and dismissing him from her life, whatever the consequences for Monteagle's future.

But her mind was still teeming with images and sensations, and it was difficult to focus somehow. To stop wondering what form his promised wooing of her might have taken. And to forget, as she must, the way he'd looked at her, the things he'd said, and—his touch. That, dear God, above all else.

Once he'd gone she'd be able to put him out of her mind, and devote herself to the on-going struggle to make Monteagle financially viable. She wouldn't have time to think about anything else—especially ludicrous might-have-beens.

She stayed awake, her brain going in weary circles, until sunlight penetrated the curtains, then dressed and went downstairs to go for a walk round the lake. Every movement was a penance, but the fresh air might help to clear her head, she told herself optimistically.

The door of the sitting room remained closed, and to her relief she had the kitchen to herself too, as she made some strong black coffee and drank it, wincing.

She stood by the water, looking across at the grey mass of Monteagle's half-ruined keep, wondering how much longer she could keep it standing without a substantial cash windfall.

Football pools, she thought. The Lottery. Quiz shows paying out thousands. What hadn't she considered in her efforts, however forlorn the hope? And now no other avenues suggested themselves.

However, she looked at it, Helen thought wretchedly, she was between a rock and a hard place.

Time was running out, and she still couldn't figure how to frame her refusal to Marc Delaroche.

With most men a simple 'I don't love you' would be enough. But he didn't want her love anyway. He wants Monteagle, she thought, her throat tightening, and maybe a son to inherit it. And a wife who'll pretend not to notice when he becomes bored and starts to stray. Or when he stops coming back altogether.

And, if I'm truly honest with myself, that's what really scares me—that I'll begin to love him because I can't help myself. That last night I felt safe and secure, for the first time in months, with his arms round me. And that in the end I'll be left alone and lonely, because that's what he does.

And I know now I couldn't bear that. It would kill me.

And that's something I can never let him guess—which is why I have to say no, once and finally.

She walked slowly back to the house. She would bathe, she thought as she went upstairs, and change. Put on a brave face.

She gave herself a little heartening nod, then flung open the bathroom door and marched in.

'*Bonjour,*' Marc said softly from the depths of the tub. He picked up the sponge and squeezed water over his head, letting it run in rivulets down his face and chest. 'Have you come to say that you will marry me? If so, you could begin your wifely duties by washing my back.'

'Oh, God,' Helen said, appalled, and backed out into the passage, slamming the door behind her to shut off the sound of his laughter.

Daisy was at the sink in the kitchen, dealing with the cups and glasses from the previous night, when Helen arrived, flushed and breathless from her headlong dash downstairs.

'Why,' she demanded, 'is Marc Delaroche still here? And what is he doing in my bathroom?'

'My guess would be—having a bath.' Daisy gave her a disapproving look. 'I dare say he could do with a bit of pampering—after last night.'

'And what's that supposed to mean?'

Daisy turned, hands on her hips, her gaze deepening into real severity. 'The very idea, Miss Helen—making the poor young man sleep on that wretched sofa when there was a perfectly good bedroom all ready for him upstairs. And Sir Henry always was such a hospitable man too. He must be turning in his grave.'

Helen took a deep breath. 'It's not a question of hospitality—' she began, but Daisy was firm.

'He told me when I saw him this morning that you were expecting him, Miss Helen. Isn't that so?'

Helen abandoned the struggle. 'Yes,' she acknowledged wearily. 'I suppose it is. I—I just wasn't sure when it would be.'

'Ah, well,' Daisy said comfortably. 'That's all right, then.' She hesitated, giving Helen a shrewd glance. 'I get the idea we'll be seeing more of Mr Marc in future.'

Helen murmured something non-committal.

I saw more than I needed just now in the bathroom, she thought, filling the kettle and placing it on the stove.

She was just making coffee when the bell at the front entrance jangled with two imperative bursts.

'Now, who on earth's calling at this time on a Sunday?' Daisy wiped her hands and moved towards the door. 'Have you invited anyone else, Miss Helen?'

'Not that I know of.' Helen attempted lightness. 'But maybe we'd better make up another room, just to be on the safe side.'

Of course it could be Lottie, curious to know how the previous evening had gone, so she turned, beaker in hand, prepared to be welcoming when Daisy returned. But the housekeeper was alone, her face set and stony. 'It's that Mr Newson,' she said shortly. 'He insists on having a word with you, so I've put him in the library.'

'Oh.' Helen abandoned her coffee and went reluctantly to join him, wishing that she looked tidier, more like the lady of the house instead of the hired help.

The room looked neat and cheerful in the sunlight pouring through the window, and her unwanted visitor was standing with his back to the empty fireplace, looking round him with his usual narrow-eyed appraisal.

She said icily, 'Is there something I can do for you, Mr Newson?'

'Yes,' he said. 'You can tell me that you've seen sense at last over this house and are prepared to sell to me. My team are all ready to go. I only need to say the word.'

'But I've already said the word.' Helen lifted her chin. 'And it's no. I thought I'd made that clear.'

'But that was when you thought you could get your hands on some money.' The fleshy face gloated at her. 'It's all round the village that you've been turned down for that grant you pinned your hopes on. You've nowhere else to turn, and you know it. So if you've got any sense you'll reconsider my offer, minus a small discount for the inconvenience you've put me to, and be quick about it. I'm planning to open next Easter.'

'Well, I hope you haven't spent too much on preliminaries,' Helen returned, with total insincerity. 'Because Monteagle is still not for sale.'

'I'm a tolerant man, Miss Frayne. Anyone will tell you that. But you're beginning to try my patience. Get it into your head, my dear. You've fought well, but you've lost. I hold all the cards, and I'm about to collect.'

Except, Helen thought, she held a final ace—if she chose to

play it. And what real choice did she have—if Monteagle was to be saved?

She heard the creak of a floorboard behind her. Knew without turning who had entered the room—and what he was waiting to hear. Her fight was over at last, and her choice made for her—whatever the consequences.

She took a deep breath, aware that she was shivering, her stomach churning as she faced Trevor Newson.

She said huskily, 'I'm afraid not. You see, I'm going to be married—very soon—and my future husband plans to restore the house completely—as our family home.' She paused. 'Isn't that right—darling?'

Marc's hands descended on her shoulders. His skin smelled cool and damp, but the lips that touched the side of her throat in a lingering kiss were warmer than the blaze of the sun.

He said softly into her ear, 'It will be one of my many pleasures, *mon amour*.'

He came to stand beside her, his arm circling her body, his hand on her hip in a gesture of possession as casual as it was disturbing. He was barefoot, bare-chested, a pair of shabby jeans his only covering.

'When I woke you were gone, *cherie*.' He clicked his tongue in a kind of amused reproach. 'And here you are, entertaining another man.'

'I don't think Mr Newson is particularly entertained,' Helen said coolly. 'Besides, he's just leaving.'

The older man's face was unpleasantly flushed. 'So this is your saviour?' He nearly spat the word. 'He doesn't look to me as if he's got two pennies to rub together, but I'm sure you've had him checked out.' He glared at Marc. 'She's a fast worker. I'll give her that. Up to yesterday she was supposed to be engaged to someone else, only he's dumped her. Now here she is with you.' Trevor Newson gave Helen a smile that made her skin crawl. 'So, where did you find this one, love?'

'She did not,' Marc said curtly. 'I found her. And you are offending my fiancée, *monsieur*. Perhaps you would like to go, before I throw you out.'

'You and whose army?' Trevor Newson blustered. He was

more heavily built than his opponent, but he was flabby and out of condition when compared with Marc's toned muscularity. 'But I'm leaving anyway.' At the door, he turned. 'This is going to cost you a fortune, my friend. I just hope you find she's worth the expense. Not many women are.'

As soon as he had gone Helen eased herself from Marc's arm and walked over to the window.

She said, 'Do you usually come downstairs half-dressed?'

'I had just finished shaving. You have some objection?' He sounded amused again.

She shrugged. 'It's—not very dignified.' She paused. 'And it made that awful man think...'

'That we had slept together?' Marc supplied cordially, as she hesitated again. 'But you can hardly deny that you spent most of the night in my arms, *ma mie.*'

'No,' Helen said between gritted teeth. 'I—can't.'

'But you wish so much that it were otherwise, *hein*?' He walked over to her. Turned her to face him, a hand under her chin, so he could look down into her eyes. 'So,' he said softly, 'you have agreed, after all, to make the ultimate sacrifice to save this house. For a while I thought your aversion to me might prove too strong.'

She bit her lip and stared down at the floor. 'So did I.' Her voice was bitter.

'I think I owe Monsieur Newson some thanks,' he said reflectively. 'If he had not come here this morning, your answer to me might have been different.'

'Yes,' she said. 'It would.' She took a deep breath. 'Don't you have any compunction about what you're doing—what you're forcing me to do? And all for a whim.' She shook her head. 'If you really want a house, there are so many others you could buy. So many women probably falling over each other to marry you.'

'But you are unique, *cherie*,' he said lightly. 'You do not profess undying love. You make it clear that you want only my money. I find that—refreshing.'

'And I,' she said in a low voice, 'find it degrading.'

He tucked an errant strand of hair behind her ear. 'Nevertheless, Hélène,' he said quietly, 'the bargain is made between us, and it will not be broken.' He dug a hand into the pocket of his jeans and produced the little velvet box. 'Now, give me your hand.'

She watched numbly as the ruby slid over her knuckle into its symbolic resting place. So beautiful, she thought, watching the slow fire that burned in its depths, and yet so totally meaningless.

He said, 'Will you give me a kiss, or do I have to take it from you?'

Swallowing nervously, she raised her mouth to his with reluctant obedience. But instead of the passionate onslaught she'd expected—and feared—Marc was gentle with her, his lips moving on hers with a strange, almost mesmerising sweetness, the tip of his tongue probing her defences softly and sensuously. Coaxing her, she thought, her mind reeling, to a response that she dared not risk—even if she wished...

She stood rigid in the circle of his arms, shakily aware of the heat of his naked skin through her clothes. Willing the kiss to end. Praying that she would escape unscathed.

At last, with a rueful sigh, he lifted his head, watching her through half-closed eyes.

'You lack warmth, *cherie*,' he told her wryly. 'But that will change once you have learned a little about pleasure.'

She stepped back from him, wrapping defensive arms round her body. 'Is that really what you think?' She invested her tone with scorn.

He laughed then, running the back of his hand teasingly down the curve of her stormy face. 'Yes, *petite innocente*, I do.' He paused, glancing at his watch. 'And now, *hélas*, I must dress and tear myself away from you back to London.'

'You're leaving?' She was genuinely astonished. 'Now?'

'*Pourquoi pas?*' He shrugged. 'After all, I have what I came for—and I have to prepare for an early meeting tomorrow.' He took the hand that wore his ring and kissed it. 'But I shall return next week. In the meantime my architect will be here, with his team, to begin restoration work on the house.'

His tone was brisk and businesslike, making her see the dynamism that drove him. See it, and resent it.

Monteagle, she thought, doesn't belong to you yet, *monsieur*.

She bristled defiantly. 'I have my own local people, thank you.'

'And now you will also have Alain.' He grinned at her. 'So, don't give him a hard time, *cherie*. He might wound more easily than I do.' He paused. 'One more thing,' he added casually. 'The number of your bank account, if you please.'

She gasped. 'Why should I give you that?'

'So that I can transfer some money for you.'

She said coldly, 'I have funds of my own, thanks. I don't need any charity.'

'And I am not offering it. But there will be incidental expenses once the work starts that you cannot be expected to meet.' He smiled at her. 'Also you have your trousseau to buy. I intend to begin the arrangements for our wedding tomorrow. I suggest a civil ceremony before witnesses at the end of next month.'

Helen's heart was thudding again. 'But you said there was no hurry,' she protested. 'That—that you'd wait...'

'I think,' he told her softly, 'that I have been patient enough already. And last night has kindled my appetite, *ma mie*.' His smile widened as he looked down into her outraged, apprehensive eyes. 'So, be good enough to write down your account number for me, and I will go and leave you in peace.'

Quivering with anger, she obeyed, handing over the slip of paper with open resentment.

Marc walked to the door, then turned slowly, letting his eyes travel down her body.

'On the other hand,' he said softly, 'I still have the memory of how you felt in my arms last night. And I could even now be persuaded to stay.'

He watched her eyes widen in sudden shock, and went on silkily, 'But it is a matter entirely for you to decide, *mon amour*. Although I promise you would find the bed in my room more comfortable than that penance of a sofa.'

The words were thick in her throat. 'I'll have to take your word for that, *monsieur*. Goodbye.'

She turned back to the window, hardly daring to breathe until she heard the door close quietly behind him.

Monteagle is safe, she whispered to herself. And that's all that matters. All that I can allow to matter, anyway.

The cost to herself—well, that was different, and she would have to find some way to endure it.

God, but he was so sure of her, she thought, digging her nails painfully into the palms of her clenched fists. So convinced he could seduce her into passionate surrender. But he would have to think again.

'You may own Monteagle, *monsieur*,' she whispered under her breath, resolution like a stone in her heart. 'But you'll never possess me—and that I swear, by everything I hold dear.'

CHAPTER SEVEN

LOTTIE looked silently at the ruby lying on the table between them.

She said, 'That's costume jewellery, and this whole thing is a wind-up—right?'

Helen shook her head. 'Wrong.' Her voice was husky. 'I really am engaged to Marc Delaroche. He—proposed last night. I accepted this morning.'

Lottie stared at her open-mouthed. She said, half to herself, 'This can't be happening. Twenty-four hours ago you considered yourself engaged to Nigel.' Her voice rose. 'And now you're going to be married to someone you've known a matter of days?'

'You made me have dinner with him,' Helen defended. 'You practically twisted my arm.'

'Yes,' said Lottie. 'Because I thought it would do you good to go out with someone lethally attractive who clearly fancied you. But that was when I thought you were both sane.'

She sat back in her chair, her worried gaze resting on Helen's pale face. 'Are we talking serious rebound from Nigel, here? Or are you telling me that love at first sight actually exists?'

'Love has nothing to do with it.' Helen drew a deep breath. 'The truth is that he's absolutely crazy about Monteagle and is willing to spend whatever it takes to restore the place to its old glory. Only it can't be completely his—unless, of course, I'm part of the package.' She shrugged. 'And that's it.'

'Oh, my God,' Lottie said helplessly, and relapsed into frowning silence. At last she said, 'Helen—just sell him the place, and save yourself a lot of heartache.'

'I'll never sell Monteagle, and he knows it. I made it clear enough at that damned committee meeting. He also knows I'm desperate.' Helen shrugged again, aiming for insouciance. 'I—

102

can't afford to refuse.' She hesitated. 'It's a business arrangement. What they call a marriage of convenience, I suppose.'

'Ah,' Lottie said blandly. 'Then presumably, as you're still virtual strangers, the deal does not include sex.' Her gaze drilled into Helen's. 'Or does it?'

Helen looked down at the table. 'We—we haven't settled the final details yet.'

'Now I know you're kidding,' said Lottie derisively. 'I saw him look at you, remember? And, while Simon and I may have been apart for a while, I still recognise old-fashioned lust when I see it. And, as you're not in love with him, how will you deal with that when payback time arrives? Are you really that sophisticated?'

Helen stared at the burn of the ruby lying between them. She said, half to herself, 'I—I'll cope somehow. Because I have to.' She forced a smile. 'What would you do in my place?'

'Sell,' said Lottie. 'And run.' She paused. 'Or you could try closing your eyes and doing exactly what you are told. That could be interesting.'

'You mean lie back and think of England?' Helen's laugh had a hollow ring. 'Or Monteagle?'

'I doubt whether Marc Delaroche will let you think about anything but him,' Lottie said drily. 'Don't say you weren't warned.'

After Lottie had gone, Helen lingered in the kitchen, washing the cups and glasses they'd used, and recorking the barely touched bottle of wine.

Daisy can use it to cheer up tomorrow's chicken casserole, she thought.

The housekeeper had taken Helen's halting news in her stride. 'So, Mr Marc, is it?' she'd said thoughtfully. 'Well, I wish you happiness, my dear. Things often turn out for the best.'

Mrs Lowell was the only other one on Helen's need-to-know list, because she'd have to explain why there'd be no more guided tours.

I'll go round to the Vicarage tomorrow, she told herself.

As she walked through the hall the telephone rang, and in spite of the lateness of the hour she found herself reaching for it.

'Hélène?' His voice reached her huskily across the miles, making her start.

She steadied herself, trying to ignore the frantic drum of her heart. 'Marc? What do you want?'

'All the things I cannot have, because you are so far from me.'

She could hear the smile in his voice and stiffened, loading her tone with frostiness. 'I mean why are you calling so late.'

'To wish you *bonne nuit*,' he said. 'And sweet dreams.'

'Oh,' she said, nonplussed. 'Well—thank you.'

'And to tell you that, to my sorrow, I will not be with you next week after all. I have to fly to New York.'

'I see.' She knew she should feel relieved at the news, if not be dancing in the streets. Instead, suddenly, there was an odd flatness. 'It was—good of you to let me know.'

There was a pause, then he said softly, 'You could go with me.'

'To New York?' An unbidden quiver of excitement stirred inside her, and was instantly quelled. She said stonily, 'Of course I can't. It's quite impossible.'

'Why? You have a passport?'

'Somewhere, yes.'

'Then I suggest you look for it, *ma mie*,' he told her drily. 'You will certainly need it for our honeymoon.'

'Honeymoon?' She was beginning to sound like an echo, she told herself with exasperation. 'But surely there's no need for that,' she protested. 'It—it's not as if it is a real marriage...'

'You will find it real enough when the time comes, *cherie*.' His words were light, but she thought she detected a note of warning. 'And we are certainly having a honeymoon—although it can only be brief because of my work commitments.'

He paused. 'An old friend has offered us his villa in the South of France. It stands on a headland above St Benoit Plage, and all the bedrooms have views of the Mediterranean. What do you think?'

'You seem to have made up your mind already,' Helen said. 'So what does it matter?'

She thought she heard him sigh. 'Then consider again about New York, Hélène. After all, how long is it since you had a holiday?'

'I went skiing with the school in my last spring term,' she said. 'That's what the passport was for.' She paused. 'But I can't just leave here. I have things to do—responsibilities. Besides...' She halted awkwardly.

'Besides, spending time alone with me in America, or anywhere, is not your idea of a vacation?' His voice was faintly caustic. 'Is that what you were about to say?'

'Something of the kind, perhaps,' Helen agreed woodenly.

'I suppose I should find your candour admirable, *ma mie*,' he said, after a pause. 'However, one day soon—or one night— we shall have to discuss your ideas in more detail.'

His tone sharpened, became businesslike. 'In the meantime, I suggest you use some of the money I shall deposit in your account to begin recruiting extra staff for the house and grounds.'

'But there's no need,' Helen protested. 'We can manage quite well as we are.'

'It is not a question of managing, *ma chère*,' Marc told her crisply. 'Monsieur and Madame Marland are no longer young, *bien sûr*, and at some point will wish to retire. In the meantime they will be glad of help, especially when there is entertaining to be done or when you are away.'

'But I'm never away,' she protested.

'Until now, perhaps,' he said. 'But that will change. You will be my wife, Hélène, not merely my housekeeper. Perhaps I have not made that sufficiently clear. When my work takes me abroad there will be times when I shall require you to go with me.'

Her voice rose slightly. 'You expect me to be your—travelling companion?'

'My companion,' he told her softly, 'and my lover. Sleeping with you in my arms was so sweet, *cherie*, that I cannot wait to repeat the experience.'

'Thank you.' She kept her voice stony, telling herself that the faint quiver she felt inside was anger. Hating the fact that she was blushing.

She took a steadying breath. 'Have you any more orders for me, or may I go now?'

He laughed. 'If I gave orders, Hélène, you would be coming with me to New York.' He gave her a second to consider that, then added more gently, 'Sleep well, *mon ange*—but think of me as you close your eyes, *hein*?'

She murmured something incoherent, and replaced the handset.

His unexpected call had shaken her, and raised issues she'd not wanted to contemplate. Questions of autonomy, among others.

It was disturbing that he seemed to want her to share his life at all kinds of levels she hadn't imagined. Starting with this—this honeymoon in the South of France. Exercising his power by taking her from her own familiar environment to his own domain, she thought, and shivered.

Slowly, she went up to her room. She took off his ring and placed it in the box which also housed her grandmother's pearls—bestowed on her for her eighteenth birthday, and the only other real valuable that she possessed.

Jewellery like the ruby didn't go with her lifestyle, and its non-stop cleaning and gardening. Nor would she take on extra staff, as he'd decreed. The arrival of his tame architect and his work crew was quite enough of an invasion of privacy, making her feel as if her personal hold on Monteagle was being slowly eroded.

But that wasn't all of it, she thought, looking down at her bare hand. There was still part of her in rebellion against the decision that had been forced on her. And she didn't want to admit to anyone, least of all herself, that both she and Monteagle would soon belong to Marc completely. Or display the symbol of that possession.

Think of me. His words came back to haunt her as she slid into bed and pulled the covers over her.

Oh, but he'd made sure of that, she thought bitterly. Turned it into an essential instead of a choice. Placed himself at the forefront of her mind each time she tried to sleep, making himself impossible to dismiss.

And when sheer fatigue overcame her, her sleep was restless and patchy, scarred by dreams that she burned with shame to remember in the morning. Dreams so real that when she woke she found herself reaching for him again across her narrow bed, before shocked realisation dawned.

She turned over, furious and humiliated, burying her heated face in the pillow.

'Damn him,' she whispered feverishly. 'Oh, damn him to hell.'

She got up, late and listless, and searched for distraction. With Daisy's assistance she finally removed the fragile bed and window hangings from the State Bedroom, folded them carefully into plastic sacks, and took them down to the village to deliver to Mrs Stevens at the post office.

The post mistress accepted them with a workmanlike glint in her eye. 'Now, this will be a real pleasure,' she said. 'We'll start on the cutting-out at once, while you decide on the new fabric.' She gave Helen a kind smile. 'So you're courting, then, Miss Frayne—that French gentleman who stayed at the Arms a while back, I hear. Met him then, did you?'

The village grapevine, Helen realised, was in full operation already.

'Oh, no,' she said with perfect truth, aware at the same time that she was blushing. 'It was before that—at a meeting in London.' *Just don't ask how long before, that's all.*

Mrs Stevens nodded with satisfaction. 'I knew it must be so,' she said.

And I wish it had been. The thought came to Helen, unbidden and shocking in its implication, as she made the short trip to the Vicarage.

'Oh, my dear girl.' Marion Lowell hugged her ebulliently. 'How amazing—a whirlwind romance. And such a gorgeous man.' She turned to her husband. 'Jeff, darling, now we have an excuse to drink that champagne we won in the Christmas tombola. I'm so glad we didn't give it back.'

'I hope none of the parishioners call,' Jeff Lowell said, grinning as he passed round the fizzing glasses. 'They'll probably have me defrocked.'

'Will you be getting married here in the church?' Mrs Lowell asked, after they'd drunk to her happiness, and Helen shook her head, flushing.

'I'm afraid not. It will be at the registry office in Aldenford.'

The Vicar looked at her quietly. 'I'd be delighted to hold a short service of blessing afterwards, if you'd like that. Perhaps you'd mention it to your fiancé.'

'Yes, of course,' said Helen, hating herself for lying.

She felt sombre as she walked home. They were so kind, so pleased for her, as if she and Marc had really fallen headlong in love.

Thank goodness they had no idea of the soulless—and temporary—bargain she'd struck with him. His words still echoed in her mind. *You do not profess undying love... I find that—refreshing.*

And that, she thought wearily, seemed to say it all.

As she rounded the bend in the road a lorry carrying scaffolding poles went past her, and carefully negotiated its way between Monteagle's tall wrought-iron gates.

She watched it bewilderedly, then began to run after it up the drive.

In front of the main entrance chaos confronted her. There seemed to be vans and trucks everywhere, with ladders and building supplies being briskly unloaded.

As she paused, staring round uncertainly, a man came striding towards her. He was of medium height, with brown hair and rimless glasses, and his face was unsmiling.

He said, 'I'm sorry, but the house is no longer open for visitors.'

'Where did you get that idea?' Helen demanded coldly.

'From Monsieur Marc Delaroche,' he said. 'The owner of the property.'

'Not yet,' Helen said with a snap. 'I'm Helen Frayne, and

the house still belongs to me.' She paused. 'I presume you're the architect?'

'Yes,' he acknowledged slowly. Behind the glasses his eyes had narrowed, as if he was puzzled about something. 'I'm Alan Graham. It's a pleasure to meet you, Miss Frayne,' he added, with no particular conviction.

'Marc mentioned you'd be coming—but not all this.' She gestured almost wildly around her. 'What's going on?'

He shrugged. 'He wants work to start as soon as possible.'

She said, 'I can see that. But how? You can't have arranged all this in twenty-four hours—it simply isn't feasible.' She stopped, dry-mouthed. 'Unless this was all planned some time ago, of course,' she added slowly. 'And you were just waiting for his word to—swing into action. Is that it?'

Alan Graham fidgeted slightly. 'Is it important? The house needs restoring, and we're here to do it. And time is of the essence,' he added with emphasis.

His tone implied that there was no more to be said. 'Is there a room I could use as an office, Miss Frayne?' He paused. 'Marc suggested that your late grandfather's study might be suitable, but any decision must be yours, naturally.'

Helen bit back the angry words seething inside her. Marc must have made his decision and given his orders almost as soon as they'd met, she realised with incredulity. As if he'd never had any doubt that she would ultimately accede to his demands.

How dare he take her for granted like this? she thought stormily, grinding her foot into the gravel in sheer humiliation. Oh, God, how dare he?

But it was done now, and she could see no way to undo it.

She took a deep breath. 'My grandfather's study has been unoccupied and unfurnished for some time,' she said expressionlessly. 'But you may use it if you wish.' She hesitated, still faintly stunned by all the activity around her. 'May I ask where all these people are going to stay?'

'That's not a problem. Accommodation has been arranged for them in Aldenford, and I've got a room at the Monteagle Arms.'

'Oh.' Helen digested this. She gave the architect a small cold smile. 'I'm afraid you won't be very comfortable there.'

'So Marc has told me.' For the first time Alan Graham's face relaxed a little. 'But it won't be for long. My wife is joining me today to look for a cottage to rent for the duration.'

'I see,' Helen said woodenly. 'And meals?' She had a horrified vision of cauldrons of soup and platters of sandwiches to be prepared daily.

'Packed lunches will be delivered.' He paused. 'Perhaps you'd direct me to the study, so that I can unpack my papers and drawings?'

'Of course,' Helen said, turning and leading the way to the house.

It seemed that Mr Graham shared Lottie's disapproval of this lightning marriage, she brooded over a mug of coffee a little later, having left the architect sorting out his workspace with chilling efficiency.

'Well!' Daisy exclaimed, bustling into the kitchen. 'You could have knocked me down with a feather when all those men started arriving. Mr Marc certainly doesn't waste any time.'

'No,' Helen agreed through gritted teeth. 'None at all.'

'They're starting on the State Bedroom,' Daisy informed her with excitement. 'The Helen Frayne portrait is being sent to London to be cleaned, and they're turning the little dressing room and the room next door as well into a lovely bathroom, with a wardrobe area.' She gave Helen a knowing look. 'Seems as if Mr Marc intends to use the room when you're married.'

'Does he, indeed?' was all Helen could find to say.

The master bedroom, she thought, her stomach twisting into nervous knots, being lavishly created for the master—and his bought bride.

When Marc telephoned that night, she was ready for him.

'You had this planned all along,' she stormed across his polite enquiries about her welfare. 'Even before you came here and saw the place you knew you were going to take on Monteagle's restoration. Why?'

'I found your application for help—intriguing. Then I saw you, *ma belle*, and my fascination was complete.' He had the gall to sound amused. 'But it seemed I had a rival, so I decided to offer you an interest-free loan in the hope that my generosity might ultimately be rewarded.'

'Then why didn't you?' Her voice was ragged.

'Because I realised that Nigel was betraying you and soon there would be nothing to prevent me claiming you for myself. It seemed unlikely that you would become my mistress, so I offered the money as a wedding gift to you instead. Do you blame me?'

'Blame you? Damned right I do,' she flung at him. 'I asked you to loan me that money—you know that. I begged you...'

'But we are both getting what we want, *mon coeur*,' he said softly. 'And that is all that matters. Why question the means?'

'Because you've deceived me,' Helen said hotly. 'You've behaved with a total lack of scruples. Doesn't that trouble you at all?'

'It is not of major concern to me, I confess,' he drawled. 'Particularly when it involves something—or someone—I desire. But if you wish it I will practise feeling ashamed for five minutes each day.'

Helen struggled to speak, failed utterly, and slammed down the phone.

He did not call her the following night, or the one after it. Gradually a week passed, and there was still silence.

And, Helen realised, she had no idea how to contact him. How ridiculous was that?

She presumed he was still in New York, and found herself wondering how he was spending his time, once work was over for the day. But that was a forbidden area, she reminded herself stonily. How Marc passed his evenings, or his nights, was none of her business. Or not until he spent them with her, of course.

Her only concern was, and always would be, Monteagle— not this ludicrously small, lost feeling that had lodged within her over the past days. There was no place for that.

All around her was a welter of dust, woodchips and falling plaster, as damp was eradicated and diseased timber ripped out amid the thud of hammers and the screech of saws and drills. Her dream was coming true at last, and Monteagle was coming slowly and gloriously back to life.

Alan Graham might still be aloof, but he knew his job, and his labour force were craftsmen who loved their work. No expense was being spared, either. Marc was clearly pouring a fortune into the project.

And that, as she kept reminding herself, was all that really mattered. She would deal with everything else when she had to.

She watched almost with disbelief as the State Bedroom was beautifully restored to its seventeenth-century origins, and, discreetly hidden behind a door, a dressing room and a glamorous twenty-first-century bathroom were created out of the adjoining room, all white and silver tiles, with a state-of-the-art shower stall and a deep sunken bathtub. Big enough for two, she noted, swallowing.

Members of the village embroidery group were already stitching the designs from the original hangings on to the pale gold fabric she'd chosen for the bed and windows, and had also promised a fitted bedcover to match.

Without the dark and tatty wallpaper, and with the lovely ceiling mouldings repaired and cleaned, and the walls painted, the huge bedroom looked incredibly light and airy, she thought. Under other circumstances it could even have been a room for happiness...

She stopped, biting her lip. Don't even go there, she told herself tersely. Happiness is a non-word.

Particularly when there had still been no contact from Marc. Clearly he was enjoying himself too much in America to bother about a reluctant bride-to-be in England.

But on the following Wednesday, while she was standing outside watching, fascinated, as the new roof went on, she heard the sound of an approaching vehicle.

She didn't look round because there always seemed to be cars and vans coming and going, until she suddenly heard Marc's voice behind her, quietly calling her name.

She turned sharply, incredulously, and saw him a few feet

away, casual in pale grey pants and a dark shirt. He held out his arms in silent command and she went to him, slowly and uncertainly, her eyes searching the enigmatic dark face, joltingly aware of the scorch of hunger in his gaze.

As she reached him he lifted her clear off the ground, and held her tightly against him in his embrace. She felt her body tremble at the pressure of his—at the pang of unwilling yearning that pierced her. Her throat was tightening too, in swift, uncontrollable excitement.

All those lonely nights, she thought suddenly, shakily, when she'd been able to think of nothing else but his touch—and, dear God, his kisses... All those restless, disturbing dreams that she was ashamed to remember.

Suddenly she wanted to wind herself around him, her arms twined about his neck, her slim legs gripping his lean hips. And realised, swiftly and starkly, the danger she was in.

As Marc's mouth sought hers she turned her head swiftly, so that his lips grazed only her cheek.

'Marc.' She tried to free herself, forcing a laugh. 'People are watching.'

He looked down into her face, his mouth hardening. 'Then that is easily remedied,' he told her softly. He lifted her effortlessly into his arms and began to carry her towards the house.

Colour stormed her face as she heard faint whistles and laughing applause from the workmen, but common sense warned her that to struggle would only make her look even more ridiculous.

Once inside, she expected to be put on her feet, but Marc carried her straight up the main staircase and along to the State Bedroom.

She said breathlessly, 'What the hell are you doing? Let me down at once.'

À votre service, mademoiselle.' His voice was cold, almost grim, as he strode across the room to the bed. Gasping, Helen found herself carelessly dropped in the middle of the wide bare mattress.

She fought herself into a sitting position, glaring at him as he stood over her, hands on hips. 'How dare you treat me like this? If you imagine I'm impressed by these—caveman tactics—then think again.'

'I should not say too much,' he told her with ominous quietness. 'It is nothing to what I would like to do to you. And will,' he added harshly, 'if you refuse my kisses again, in public or in private, no matter what grudge you may be harbouring.'

She bit her lip, avoiding the starkness of his dark gaze. 'You—you took me by surprise. I wasn't expecting to see you.'

'*Évidemment,*' he said caustically. 'Is that why you are not wearing my ring?'

Of course he would have to notice that!

'I'm living on a building site,' Helen returned a touch defensively. 'I didn't want it to get lost or damaged.'

He gave her a sceptical glance. 'Or did it remind you too much of how soon you will be my wife?'

She bit her lip. 'What do you expect—eager anticipation?'

'No,' he said softly. 'But if not a welcome—a little co-operation, perhaps?'

Before she could move she felt his hands on her shoulders, pushing her back on to the mattress again. Then, lifting himself lithely on to the bed beside her, he pulled her close, and his lips began to explore her mouth with cool, almost languorous pleasure.

Taking, she realised, all the time in the world.

Her hands came up against his chest, trying to maintain at least some distance between them, but that was all the resistance she dared attempt. His warning still rang in her mind, and she knew she could not afford to provoke him again. She would have been wiser to offer him her lips in front of everyone just now rather than risk this.

She was too vulnerable, she thought, shut away with him here in this room they'd soon be sharing. And, because they were known to be together, no one would be tactless enough to come looking for them. No one...

The midday sun was pouring in through the high windows, lapping them in heated gold.

She seemed to be sinking helplessly, endlessly, down into the softness of the bed, her lips parting in spite of herself to answer the sensuous pressure of his mouth, to yield to the silken invasion of his tongue.

Inside her thin shirt, her breasts were suddenly blossoming in greedy delight as his kiss deepened in intensity. Her hardening nipples seemed tormented by the graze of the lacy fabric that enclosed them, aching to be free of its constriction.

As if she'd moaned her yearning aloud, she felt his hand begin gently to unfasten the buttons on her shirt.

She lay still, scarcely breathing, the sunlight beating on her closed eyelids, her pulses frantic, waiting—waiting…

Marc was kissing her forehead, brushing the soft hair away from her temples with his lips, discovering the delicate cavity of her ear with his tongue, then feathering caresses down her arched throat to the scented hollow at its base, where he lingered.

His fingers slid inside the open neck of her shirt, pushing it and the thin strap beneath away from her shoulder.

Then he bent his head, and she experienced for the first time the delicious shock of a man's lips brushing the naked swell of her breast above the concealing lace of her bra, and knew that she wanted more—so much more that it scared her.

She made a small sound, half-gasp, half-sob. For a moment he was very still, then suddenly, unbelievably, she felt him lift himself away from her.

When she had the power to open her dazed eyes she saw that he was standing beside the bed, almost briskly tucking his own shirt back into the waistband of his pants.

'Je suis désolé,' he said. 'But I have arranged to see Alain for his progress report, and I am already late.'

Helen felt as if she'd been hit by a jet of freezing water. She scrambled up on to her knees, feverishly cramming her shirt buttons back into their loops. Restoring herself to decency with a belated attempt at dignity.

Her voice shook a little. 'I apologise if I've caused you any inconvenience.'

'*Au contraire,*' he said, his smile glinting at her. '*Tu es toute ravissante.*'

Anger began to mingle with shock inside her as she met his gaze. The victor, she thought stormily, with his spoils. And she'd nearly—nearly—let him...

She should have been the one to draw back, not him, she realised with shame. Oh, God, how could she have been such a fool?

He paused, glancing at his watch. 'But the report should not take long,' he went on softly, outrageously. 'Perhaps you would like to wait here for my return?'

'No,' Helen said between her teeth. 'I would not.'

One of her shoes had fallen off, and she began to search for it with her bare foot.

'*Quel dommage,*' he commented. 'I hoped you would show me round the rest of the house. Let me know what you think of the work that has been done so far and of any changes you would like to make.'

'I'm sorry,' Helen said icily, 'but we no longer provide guided tours. And the only change I want is never to see you again.'

He had the gall to grin at her. 'How fickle you are, *cherie*. When only a moment ago...' He shrugged and gave an exaggerated sigh.

'But your mention of tours has reminded me,' he added more slowly. 'As I drove here I met Madame Lowell in the village. She asked if you had told me of her husband's offer to bless our marriage. I said you had not been able to contact me, but that it was a great kindness of Révérend Lowell, which we would be delighted to accept.'

'You said *what*?' Helen abandoned the hunt for her shoe and stared at him, bright spots of colour flaring in her pale face. 'How could you do that? How could you? The Lowells are a sweet couple, and they really believe in marriage. Genuine marriage, that is,' she added, her voice stinging. 'It's sheer hypocrisy to involve them in our—sordid little bargain.'

His mouth tightened. He said harshly, all trace of amusement fled, 'Perhaps, *ma mie*, I feel that in spite of what has taken place between us here our—bargain needs all the help it can get.'

He took her by the shoulders, jerking her off the edge of the bed towards him, and his mouth was hard on hers in a kiss which bore no relation to his earlier tenderness.

It was, Helen thought, her mind reeling, almost a punishment.

When he released her, his eyes were glittering as they studied her startled face. Her hand went up mechanically to cover her tingling lips.

He said, 'So, understand this, Hélène: our marriage will be as genuine as anyone could wish—in all the ways that matter.' His voice was ice. 'On that, *ma belle*, you have my solemn word.'

He walked away from her across the big room, opening a space like an abyss between them. And left, slamming the door behind him.

CHAPTER EIGHT

HELEN stood, her hand still pressed to her mouth, as she tried to calm her flurried breathing.

She heard herself whisper raggedly, 'I—should not have said that.'

But she could not deny she'd wanted to make him angry—even to hurt him. She'd wanted revenge for his staying away in silence—for her dreams and her loneliness—and most of all for the way his hands and mouth had made her feel. Only revenge hadn't been so sweet after all.

Nor had he been angry enough to call off the marriage. And for Monteagle's sake she should be thankful for that.

She pushed her tangled hair back from her face and walked slowly to the door.

It might be politic to make some kind of amends, however. Not go to the lengths of an apology, of course. But perhaps if she prepared his room herself—put flowers in it?

She got sheets and pillowcases from the linen cupboard and carried them to the room he'd used briefly before. She opened a window to let in the sunlight and the faint breeze, wrinkling her nose at the sound of the building work, then quickly made up the bed, the pillows plumped and the sheets immaculately smooth.

She was coming back from the garden, her hands full of roses, when as she rounded the house she heard Alan Graham say, 'What are you going to do about Angeline Vallon?'

Helen halted, puzzled, then realised his voice was coming from the open window of her grandfather's study, just above her head.

Marc, she thought, shrinking against the cover of the wall. He must be talking to Marc. And felt her whole body tense.

118

She strained her ears, but couldn't catch the quietly spoken reply.

Then the other man spoke again. 'Marc—she's not a problem that will simply vanish. And she's bound to have heard by now that you're to be married. There could be trouble.' He paused. 'And your *fiancée* might find out.'

'Then I shall take care she does not.' Marc must have come to the window too, because, for her sins, she could hear him clearly now. And regretted it with all her heart.

'You worry too much, *mon ami*,' he went on. 'I will deal with Angeline—and that jealous fool she is married to if I have to. And Hélène need know nothing.'

Helen felt frozen. She was terrified in case Marc glanced down and saw her there below—eavesdropping—and knew she could not risk staying where she was a moment longer. Besides, she couldn't stand to hear any more.

I ought to be glad that there's another woman in his life. Relieved that our marriage is of such little importance to him, she told herself brokenly. But I'm not—*I'm not*...

Slowly and carefully, she tiptoed back to the house, pausing only to thrust the roses into one of the bins by the back door.

Some of the thorns, she saw, had drawn blood from her hands. But what she'd just overheard seemed to be draining the blood from her heart.

Because she realised she could never let him see how much this painfully acquired secret knowledge was hurting her. Nor dared she ask herself why this should be so. Her instinct told her that the answer she sought might be beyond all bearing.

The dress wasn't white, Helen told herself defensively. It was ivory. A major difference when it came to symbolism. But it was still her wedding dress, and in little more than an hour she would wear it as she stood in Aldenford registry office and became Marc Delaroche's wife.

Time had run out at last, and she was frightened.

Her hair, which had been skilfully layered and highlighted, framed a face that looked pale and strained in spite of the best efforts of the beautician who'd just left.

Also reflected in her mirror was the set of elegant matching luggage on the bed, containing the trousseau that Lottie, once she'd become convinced that Helen would not turn back from her chosen course, had relentlessly forced her into buying.

Including, of course, this slim-fitting dress in heavy silk. The skirt reached just below her knees, and the bodice was cut square across her breasts with slender shoestring straps, now hidden discreetly under the matching jacket, waist-length, mandarin-collared, and fastened with a dozen or more tiny silk-covered buttons.

It was beautiful, thought Helen, and in truth she hadn't needed much persuading to buy it.

Lottie had approved of the evening and cocktail dresses, the casual day clothes and beachwear that Helen had reluctantly selected.

'Don't be such a Puritan,' she'd urged. 'You're marrying a multimillionaire and going on honeymoon to one of the smartest resorts on the Riviera. Marc will expect you to dress—and undress—accordingly.'

'Why are you on his side all of a sudden?' Helen had asked, flushing.

'I'm on your side.' Lottie had given her a swift hug. 'Which is why I'm determined that you'll do yourself credit.'

She'd pulled a face at Helen's choice of lingerie, in crisp white cotton and broderie anglais, and raised her eyebrows at the nightgowns too, demurely simple in pale silk, and cut severely on the bias.

'Expecting fire to break out?' she'd teased, probably puzzled that there was no lace, no chiffon. Nothing sheer or overtly sexy.

But for that, thought Helen, wincing, Marc had someone else.

Even if she hadn't heard that betraying snatch of conversation she would have guessed as much by now. Because since those brief delirious moments she'd spent in his arms, and their angry aftermath, Marc had not made the slightest attempt to be alone with her, or to touch her—apart from a formal brush of his lips across her cheek on greeting or leavetaking. And sometimes not even that.

Nor had he spent a single night at Monteagle in the room

she'd made ready for him, choosing instead, on his flying visits, to stay with Alan and Susan Graham at Lapwing Cottage.

But that would end tonight. In a matter of hours they would be alone together in a starlit room overlooking the Mediterranean. And she supposed that in spite of the coldness between them he'd expect her to share his bed, submit to whatever demands he made of her.

Although that same chill might spare her the seductive persuasion he'd used the last time she was in his arms. There had been little defence she'd been able to summon against that, she thought, her throat tightening as she recalled her body's naïve response—and his almost amused rejection.

But tonight she would be on her guard, fighting ice with ice.

For the sake of her emotional sanity she had to try, anyway. Because this was the price she had to pay for Monteagle, and there was no escaping it.

Unless Marc himself let her go. And she could always hope— couldn't she?

Helen was shocked to find the parish church full as she walked up the aisle, her hand reluctantly in Marc's.

A lot of people were there, she knew, because they were simply curious to take a look at the French millionaire who'd swept young Helen Frayne off her feet. Probably quite a few were disappointed because she wasn't wearing a white crinoline with a veil. But the majority had just come to wish her well. She could feel the waves of goodwill rolling towards her as she stood at the altar with her bridegroom, and she felt the colour deepen in her face.

Oh, God, she thought. The blushing bride. What a cliché.

She wanted to turn and tell them, Don't be fooled. I'm a total fraud and this marriage is strictly business.

Up to that moment things had passed almost in a blur. The formal phrases uttered by the registrar in Aldenford a short while before had hardly impinged on her consciousness. But now the gleam of Marc's wedding ring on her hand was a cogent reminder that the deed was done.

She was aware that Marc had turned slightly to look at her,

and kept her own gaze trained on Jeff Lowell's kind face. She didn't want to see what might or might not be in her new husband's eyes.

When they'd met at the registrar's office, he had told her quietly that she looked very beautiful. He looked amazing too, she thought with a pang, the elegant dark suit doing more than justice to his tall, lean body. But naturally she hadn't said so. Instead she'd thanked him with equal politeness for the cream and yellow roses he'd sent her.

She'd been aware of Lottie looking anxious, and of Alan Graham's tight smile as they stepped forward to act as witnesses for the brief ceremony.

Now she stood taut as wire, the Vicar's serious words on God's gift of love reaching her from some far distance. She found herself wondering what he meant—questioning what relevance his words bore to her confused and panic-stricken situation.

This is wrong, she thought, her throat tightening. What we're doing is so wrong...

She knelt at Marc's side to receive the blessing, and realised with surprise that he had made the sign of the cross as it was pronounced.

As they rose, Marc took her hand and turned her towards him. He said quietly, *'Ma femme.'*

She knew he was going to kiss her, and that this time there could be no protest or evasion. Silently she raised her mouth to his, allowing his lips to possess hers with a warm and lingering tenderness she had not expected. And if she did not respond he was the only one who knew it.

At the same time Helen was aware of a faint stir in the congregation. No doubt they were pleased to see the romantic myth fulfilled, she thought, torn between irony and bleakness.

Still clasping her hand, Marc led her down the aisle, courteously acknowledging the congratulations and good wishes from all sides.

And then Helen, halfway to the sunlit doorway, understood the reason for that sudden restlessness behind them. Because

Nigel was there, leaning against the wall at the back, smiling thinly as he watched them approach.

For a moment she thought she was having a hallucination—a waking nightmare. Because he was the last person she wanted to see—and what was he doing there, anyway? What could he possibly want?

She cast a fleeting glance up at Marc and saw his face become a coolly smiling mask just as his fingers tightened round hers.

Their car was waiting at the lych gate to take them to the airport, and suddenly she wanted to run to it. To be inside it and away without any further leavetaking or good wishes from anyone.

But there was no chance of that. People were pouring out of the church around them, and a lot had cards and lucky silver horseshoes to bestow, while even more seemed to have cameras.

Helen stood, smiling composedly until her facial muscles felt stiff. At some moment Marc must have relinquished her hand, because they'd become separated. Looking round for him, she saw he was standing a few yards away with Alan, enigmatically receiving rowdy advice from some of the local men.

'Do I get to kiss the bride?' Nigel's voice beside her was soft and insinuating, but the arms that pulled her into his embrace held no gentleness. Nor was there any kiss. Instead, his cheek pressed against hers in a parody of a caress as he whispered into her ear, 'If the conversation flags tonight, sweetie, why not ask him about Angeline Vallon? And see if he tells you.'

She pulled herself free, pain slashing at her. I don't need to ask, she wanted to scream at him. I already know.

But Nigel had already gone, melting into the laughing crowd.

Instead, she saw Marc coming towards her, his face granite-hard.

He said curtly, 'I think it is time we left, Hélène. *Allons.*'

And silently, shakily, she obeyed.

Their silence during the ride to the airport had continued during the flight to the South of France.

Marc had apologised briefly for having work to do. 'But once it is completed I shall be able to devote myself to you,' he'd added, slanting a coolly sardonic smile at her before becoming immersed in papers from his briefcase.

Helen's heart had lurched uneasily, but she'd made no reply. Instead she sipped the champagne she was offered, and stared out of the window.

The flight should have provided some kind of respite from the stress of the day, but not when the name Angeline Vallon was buzzing in her brain.

The fact that she was Marc's current mistress must be common knowledge if Nigel was aware of it. Common sense suggested that she should confront her husband on the subject, letting him know she was not the innocent dupe he clearly imagined.

Yet some instinct told her that she had reached a threshold she should not cross. After all, Marc had never promised to be faithful, she reminded herself painfully. And it might even make her life easier if his physical demands were being satisfied elsewhere and she became simply his official wife, to be produced in public when required and left to her own devices in the country at all other times.

All she really needed was—somehow—to make her life bearable again.

Although her immediate concern, she realised, dry-mouthed, was to get through the week ahead of her—and particularly the next twelve hours of it.

She sat tensely beside Marc in the back of the chauffeur-driven car which had met them at the airport. It was already sunset, and lights were coming on all along the Promenade des Sables at St Benoit Plage, illuminating the marina, with its plethora of expensive yachts, and the up-market boutiques, bars and cafés that lined the other side of the thoroughfare.

Behind the promenade terraces of houses rose steeply to be crowned by a floodlit pale pink building with a dome, which Helen thought was a church until Marc informed her with faint amusement that it was the town's casino.

'Would you care to go there one evening?' he asked. 'There is an excellent restaurant, and you could try your luck at the tables.'

'Thank you, but, no,' she refused curtly. 'My father was the gambler of the family. I don't want to follow in his footsteps.'

He shrugged slightly. 'As you wish,' he returned. 'Then I shall go alone.'

The Villa Mirage occupied its headland in splendid isolation and was reached by a narrow snaking road. It was large and rambling, built on two storeys, and surrounded by a broad terrace at ground level. The first floor rooms were served by communal balconies, each with a flight of steps that led down to the luxuriant gardens, and bougainvillaea tumbled over the white walls.

In other circumstances she'd have been entranced. Now she was just scared.

The owners, Thierry and Nicole Lamande, were abroad on an extended business trip, Marc had told her, and they would be looked after by the staff, Gaston and Elise.

'I hope,' he'd added ironically, 'that you will not find it too secluded.'

Gaston turned out to be a taciturn man with a grave smile—in direct contrast to his wife, who was small and ebullient with a mass of greying hair. Chattering volubly, she conducted Helen upstairs to a large room at the back of the house, overlooking the swimming pool, with its own dressing room and elegantly appointed bathroom.

Gaston followed with her luggage, but, to her surprise, Helen realized that Marc's bags, brought up by the chauffeur, were being placed in an identical room just across the passage. And presumably by Marc's own order.

So the immediate pressure seemed to be off, she thought, suppressing a gasp of relief.

All the same, she tried to ignore the wide bed, with its immaculate white-embroidered linen, as she walked across to the long windows that led to the balcony and opened the shutters. The air was warm and still, carrying a faint fragrance of lavender from one of the local flower farms, while the rasp of cicadas filled the gathering dusk.

She took a long, luxurious breath, trying to calm herself. 'It's going to be all right,' she whispered. 'Everything's going to be fine.'

She turned to re-enter the bedroom, and halted with a stifled cry. Because Marc was there, leaning in the doorway, arms folded as he watched her.

She said unevenly, 'You—you startled me.'

'You seem easily alarmed, *ma mie*.' His mouth twisting derisively, he came forward into the room. 'I have only been asked to say that our dinner will be ready in twenty minutes.'

'Oh,' she said, trying to sound pleased when she'd never felt less hungry in her life. 'Then I'll come down.' She turned away, beginning to fumble with the little satin-covered buttons on her jacket, trying to drag them free from their loops.

'Be careful,' he said. 'Or they will tear.' He walked over to her and removed her shaking hands from their task, dealing with the fastenings himself, deftly and impersonally.

She'd planned to take the jacket off, of course, but she felt absurdly self-conscious as she slipped it from her shoulders—as if, she thought, she was suddenly naked under his inscrutable dark gaze.

'Your dress is charming,' he said, after a pause that seemed to Helen's overwrought senses to have lasted fractionally too long. 'Perhaps we should give a party when we return to England, so that all your friends in the village can admire its true glory. What do you think?'

She shrugged as she walked past him towards the door. 'I'm sure people will want to see how the house is progressing, anyway,' she returned quietly. 'But won't you find a village party rather boring?'

His brows lifted. 'With you beside me, *cherie*?' he asked mockingly. 'Impossible. Now, let us go and eat our wedding supper.'

A table had been set for them under an awning on the terrace, bright with tiny bowls of scented flowers and candles in little glass shades. Gaston brought Helen the dry white wine she'd asked for, while Marc drank Ricard.

The food was wonderful, even though Helen was fully aware she was not doing it justice. A delicately flavoured vegetable terrine was followed by poached sole, then tiny chickens simmered in wine and grapes. After the cheese came *milles-feuilles*, thick with liqueur-flavoured cream.

Helen was sparing with the excellent Chablis offered with the meal, and, to Marc's open amusement, resolutely refused the brandy that arrived with the tall silver coffeepot.

'Afraid that it will send you to sleep again, *ma chère*?' His brows lifted. 'I promise it will not.'

Her heart lurched. 'Did Elise do all of this?' she asked, keen to change the subject. 'She's a miraculous cook.'

'A lot of people would agree.' He smiled faintly. 'And many attempts have been made to lure her away, but she remains faithful to Thierry and Nicole.'

She said stiltedly, 'It was kind of them to lend you this beautiful house.'

'And I am sorry we have only a week, instead of the month they offered,' he returned. 'But it may be that we can go on a longer trip later in the year—to the Caribbean, perhaps, or the Pacific islands.' He paused. 'Would you like that?'

She didn't look at him. 'It—it sounds wonderful.'

Oh, stop pretending, she begged silently. *Please, stop pretending.*

It was growing very late, she realised. The deep indigo of the sky was sparked with stars, and a slight breeze had risen, carrying with it the murmur of the sea.

She suddenly realised she was going to yawn, and tried desperately to mask it with her hand. But he noticed.

'Tu es fatiguée?'

'No—not at all.' Her denial was too swift—too emphatic. 'It's so lovely here,' she added, forcing a smile. 'I'm trying to take it all in.'

'That may be easier in daylight. And I am glad that you are not tired.' Marc finished his brandy and rose. He came round to her and extended his hand. 'It is time for bed, *ma femme*,' he said softly. *'Viens.'*

Shakily, Helen got to her feet and let him lead her into the house, across the shadows of the *salon* and up the stairs beyond.

At her door, Marc paused, running a rueful hand over his chin. 'I need to shave,' he told her. 'So I will join you presently.'

Swallowing, Helen backed into her room and closed the door. The lamps had been lit on either side of the bed, and the covers were turned down. One of her nightgowns—the white one—was waiting for her, fanned out over the foot of the bed.

So she was not to be spared after all, she thought numbly. Even though there was another woman in his life, Marc was still not prepared to forego the novelty of possessing his virgin bride.

It had been bad enough when she'd only had the danger of her own responses to fight, she thought. But now she had the added humiliation of knowing that she would be sharing him. That even on their wedding night she'd be denied the small comfort of knowing that, for a brief time, he'd been hers alone.

A laugh like a sob escaped her. 'My God,' she whispered. 'And I thought I could fight him.'

She went over to the dressing table and sank down on the padded stool. In the lamplight she looked pale, her eyes wide and almost bruised.

She thought, How can I bear this? What shall I do? And sat motionless, her face buried in her hands.

She did not hear the door open, but some deep instinct warned her when she was no longer alone. She raised her head and met his gaze in the mirror. He was standing behind her, wearing a robe of dark silk which she knew would be his only covering.

He had showered as well, she realised. The clean damp scent of his skin filled her senses, and she took a swift breath of helpless longing.

He said quietly, 'I thought you would be in bed, *ma belle*.'

'My dress,' she said, snatching at an excuse. 'I—I couldn't reach…'

'You could have come to me, Hélène. Asked me to help you.' His hands closed on her shoulders, urging her gently to her feet. 'Like this,' he whispered.

Helen felt the tiny hook on her bodice give way, and the faint rasp of the zip as he lowered it. She felt his mouth touch the nape of her neck, then move with sure gentleness to her shoulder, pushing away the thin strap, baring the soft skin for his lips.

She felt the dress begin to slip down her body, and clutched it with both hands as the first dangerous and uncontrollable tremor of need quivered through her body.

He turned her slowly to face him, his mouth seeking hers. He said softly, *'Mon ange.'*

Angel, she thought dazedly, her pulses swimming. My angel. My—Angeline… Was that what he called her too—*mon ange*? Were these the caresses he used to seduce his mistress—and countless others?

Marc's women—so easily interchangeable. So soon forgotten.

But only if she allowed it, she told herself, anger building on wretchedness.

As he kissed her she turned her face away sharply, so that his mouth grazed only her cheek. In a voice she didn't recognise, she said, 'No—no, Marc, please.'

He paused, frowning, but more in surprise than annoyance. His hands cupped her face, making her look at him. *'Qu'as tu?'* His tone was still gentle. 'What is the matter?'

'I can't do this.' She swallowed. 'I thought I—could. But it's impossible.'

He put his arms round her, his hands slipping inside the loosened dress, gently stroking the naked vulnerability of her back, making her shiver and burn.

'Mon amour,' he murmured, as if he sensed her body's confusion. 'There is nothing to fear. Do you think I would hurt you? I promise I shall not.'

But she was in pain already. She screamed at him soundlessly. She occupied an agonising wasteland where need fought with reason and heartbreak and humiliation waited to devour her like hungry tigers. And if she turned to him now, she would be lost.

'Please—you have to let me go.' Her voice cracked. 'I—I can't be what you want—do what you want. You—you said you'd be patient…'

'Patient,' he repeated, almost incredulously. 'You dare to say that to me? *Mon Dieu!* When have I not been patient? Even when your body was mine for the taking, I held back. Waited for the moment when you would be my wife in honour.'

'There is no honour,' Helen said, her voice a shaken breath. 'We—made a deal. That's all.'

Grim-faced, he stepped back from her. *'Mais, oui,'* he said. 'We had a deal—that sordid little bargain of ours, to which you agreed, *ma chère*, however much you may regret it at this moment.'

She faced him, her arms wrapped round her body. 'You threw me a lifeline,' she said. 'And I was grateful. I didn't let myself consider—the personal implications. At least, not until now.'

'Not even when you were in my arms, *ma belle*?' His laugh was harsh. His words seared her to the core. 'I think you are lying.' He paused. 'But here is something else for you to consider. Why should I continue to keep to the terms of our agreement if you do not?'

There was a silence. At last she said hoarsely, 'You mean you'd—abandon Monteagle? Stop all the work because I—I won't...'

She stared at him pleadingly, but found she was looking into the narrowed angry eyes of a stranger.

She said, stammering slightly, 'But you couldn't do that, surely? You—you love it too much. Besides, you promised...'

'And you,' he said, 'made a vow also. Just today. And, whatever I feel about the house, I hate being cheated far more, *ma petite trompeuse*. And if you can break your word so easily, then so can I.'

He paused. 'Or maybe you would prefer to—reconsider, my beautiful wife. After all, we still have the rest of the night. And surely for the sake of your beloved Monteagle you can endure this—minor inconvenience. But do not make me wait too long for your decision,' he added coldly, turning away. 'And this time, *madame*, you will come to me.'

Helen stood motionless, hardly breathing as she watched the door close behind him.

After a while she unclasped her arms and let the dress slide to the ground. She stepped out of it and went into the bathroom, running water into the tub as she took off her underwear and put it in the linen basket.

Then she climbed into the bath and lay back, closing her eyes, trying to be calm—rational.

All over the world, she thought, women were having sex when they didn't want to. That was nothing new. She couldn't, of course, fake an orgasm. Even if she knew how she guessed Marc would not be deceived for a moment. Instead, she would have to feign the frigidity that Nigel had once accused her of. Maintain some kind of integrity by her indifference, no matter what the cost—and instinct told her it would be high.

This minor inconvenience, he'd said, his mouth twisting cynically.

Oh, God, she whispered wretchedly. How little he knew.

She could only hope he would soon become bored by her passive resistance. But until then...

She dried herself, cleaned her teeth and brushed her hair. Calming herself with the usual routine of bedtime.

She went over to the bed, picked up the pretty, fragile thing that lay there, and slipped it on over her head. She supposed he would want her to take it off. Supposed, but did not know. Not for certain. Nothing for certain.

It's ludicrous, she thought, swallowing a small, fierce sob. My first time with a man and I haven't a bloody clue.

Except, of course, the remembrance of his hands weaving their dark magic on her skin only a short time before. The magic she'd always known could be her downfall.

The white silk rustled faintly above her bare feet as she went slowly out of the room and across the passage. The door of his room was ajar, and she pushed it open and stepped into the lamplit silence.

CHAPTER NINE

MARC was lying propped up on an elbow, facing the door. Waiting, she realised, without one solitary doubt for her to appear. Savouring his victory in advance. The enjoyment he so confidently expected.

Yet there was no triumph in the brief, bleak smile he accorded her.

He pulled back the cover, indicating without words that she should join him. Helen obeyed, lying rigid and awkward beside him, aware of the painful thud of her heart, but even more conscious of his naked warmth and the grave dark eyes studying her face.

Still propped on his elbow, Marc lifted his other hand, stroking the hair back from her temples with his fingertips, then moving down to trace the arch of her eyebrows. His touch was as light as the brush of a butterfly's wing as it followed the hollows of her cheekbones, then hovered at the corner of her mouth.

'Hélène.' His voice was oddly gentle too. 'Do you know how I have longed for this moment—and for you?'

He bent his head and kissed her, his lips moving coaxingly on her unresponsive mouth while his hand slid down to the demure neckline of her nightdress, brushing its straps off her shoulders.

'C'est très jolie, ça,' he whispered. 'But I think you would be even lovelier without it.'

She was shaking inside as the silk slipped down her body, and she heard his soft murmur of satisfaction as his fingers cupped her bare breast. No matter how determined she might be to withstand him, she found with dismay that she could not prevent her nipple hardening in excitement at his caress, or deny the sudden languorous melting between her thighs.

Marc bent towards her again, his mouth closing on the rounded softness he'd uncovered, his tongue laving its engorged peak with passionate finesse.

He was lying beside her now, his arm round her shoulders, holding her against him, leaving her in no doubt that he was fiercely aroused. His hand drifted slowly downwards over her body, exploring each curve and contour through the thin fabric of her nightdress, creating a delicate, enticing friction against her skin.

She felt his fingers linger on her hipbone, then move inwards across the flat plane of her stomach with unmistakable purpose while his mouth sought hers with renewed intensity.

She moved then, swiftly, frantically, both hands capturing his and dragging it away from her body. 'Don't,' she said hoarsely. 'Don't touch me.'

He was still for a moment, then she heard him sigh.

'Ah, mon amour.' He took her hand and raised it to his lips, caressing her palm softly. 'Don't fight me, *je t'en supplié*. Relax. Let me make this beautiful for you.'

'Beautiful?' She echoed the word with bitter incredulity. 'You bought me for sex, *monsieur*, so how can it possibly be beautiful? Not that it matters. I—just want it to be over.'

He was suddenly tense, his fingers gripping hers almost painfully. At last he said quietly, 'Hélène, you do not know what you are saying.'

'Yes—yes, I do.' The words tumbled out of her, heartsick and wounded. 'I'm sick of this hypocrisy—this pretence that I'm anything more to you than just another girl in another bed, marriage or no marriage. And I can't bear to be touched—kissed,' she added quickly. 'So just—do it and let me go. Because I don't want you and I never will.'

His sudden harsh laugh made her flinch. He released her and sat up, the sheet falling away from his body, his mouth grim. 'And what now, *madame*? I am expected, perhaps, to admit defeat and send you back to the virgin sanctity of your room. Is that it? To be followed by a swift, discreet annulment back in England?'

He shook his head. 'Well, you may dream on, *mon coeur*.

Because you will go nowhere until I have made our marriage a reality.'

Before she even realised what was happening he had lifted himself over her, his hand pushing back her nightgown and parting her thighs with ruthless determination.

She felt his fingers discover the moist silken heat that he'd created, in spite of herself, heard him laugh softly, and could have died of shame.

'You'll make me hate you,' she stormed, trying to twist away from him and failing totally.

'That is your privilege,' he said. 'This—is mine.' And, poised above her, slowly, skilfully, he guided himself into her.

She lay beneath him unmoving, hardly able to breathe, her eyes closed and one fist pressed against her mouth, waiting for the pain but determined that she would not cry out.

Yet there was no need. She had not expected consideration. Probably did not deserve gentleness. But he offered them to her just the same. In spite of the unyielding tautness of her body, his possession of her was deliberately leisured and totally complete. Also utterly determined.

Yet at the same time it was a curiously sterile performance. Sexually naïve as she was, Helen could still recognise that. And although she'd stipulated no kisses or caresses she'd not expected him to listen. But it seemed that he had, because apart from that one supreme intimacy of his body joined to hers there was no other physical contact between them. His weight was supported by his arms, clamped either side of her on the bed.

When he began to move, it was also without haste. The drive of his body was controlled and clinical, expressing an almost steely resolve, and when Helen risked a scared, fleeting glance upwards at his face she saw that it was set and expressionless, his gaze fixed on the wall above the bed. As if he had withdrawn behind some silent, private barricade.

And even as she realised with anguish, This is not—*not* how it should be...she felt, deep within her, at that moment, a small stirring, as if the petals of a flower were slowly unfurling in the sunlight. But as her shocked mind acknowledged it, tried with a kind of desperation to focus there, it was gone.

At the same time she heard his breathing change suddenly, and felt his body convulse violently inside hers as he reached his climax.

She heard him cry out something that might almost have been her name, his voice hoarse and ragged, as if that unyielding wall of reserve had suddenly crumbled, and for an instant she felt his weight slump against her, pressing her down into the bed.

But he released himself almost at once and rolled away from her, burying his face in his folded arms so that she was free.

For a while she lay still, adjusting to the slight soreness between her thighs and knowing at the same time that it did not compare with the vast ache of loneliness and frustration that now filled her bewildered body, making her want to moan aloud.

She moved away a little, towards the edge of the bed. She said, dry-mouthed, 'May I go now—back to my own room?'

For a long moment there was silence, then slowly he raised his head and looked at her, his face wearily sardonic. '*Pourquoi pas?* Why not? I assume you do not wish to sleep in my arms and have me kiss you awake in the morning. So go back to your sanctuary, my little cheat.'

His words stung, especially when she knew that even now, if he reached for her—held her—she would not be able to resist him.

She lifted her chin. 'I hardly cheated. I did what you expected.'

'Did you?' His mouth twisted. 'How little you know, *cherie*.' He shrugged a sweat-slicked shoulder. 'And I still say you are a cheat. Because your victim is now yourself. You have defrauded your own body of the warmth and passion of being a woman. And you did it deliberately. Or did you think I would not know?' he added with contempt. 'So sleep with that, *hein*?'

Somehow Helen got back to her own room. Somehow she stripped off her crumpled nightdress, kicking it away, and turned on the shower, letting the warm water rain down on her in a torrent, mingling with the sudden tears on her face.

She whispered brokenly, 'It could have been worse. It could have been so much worse...'

And knew that she was lying.

It was late when Helen came back to full consciousness the next morning. She'd eventually fallen into an uneasy sleep around dawn, but now the sunlight was burning through the shutters, she realised, shading dull eyes with her hand as she peered at the window.

And somehow she had to shower, dress, and go downstairs to face Marc, she thought, uttering a soft groan at the prospect.

Yet at least she'd woken alone, and not been roused by his kisses, she told herself, remembering with a pang his soft-voiced taunt of the night before, as she pushed away the tangled sheet and swung her feet to the floor.

His accusation that she'd cheated herself of fulfilment still rankled bitterly, however, and her body was haunted by a feeling of numb emptiness that almost amounted to desolation.

Inexperienced as she was, her inner desolation was not helped by the recognition that her husband had subjected her to a possession without passion—a disciplined and calculated exercise for his own satisfaction. Nor was it alleviated by the knowledge that she'd deliberately instigated this bleak and untender consummation.

Was this a foretaste of what she could expect each night of this caricature of a honeymoon? she wondered. If so, at least it would make it marginally easier to withhold herself, as she knew she must.

She had to be careful too, she thought, remembering that brief instant when simply the stark rhythm of his body inside hers had been enough to provoke that strange flicker of desire, as unwelcome as it was unexpected, but no less potent for that.

She could only hope that, caught between boredom and anger in this war of attrition between them, Marc would be keen to put the whole wretched episode behind him and return to his former way of life—and the women who shared it. Once this painful pretence of a marriage was finished in any significant way, she might be able to attain some peace.

After all, she thought, swallowing, Marc still had the house, which was and always had been his main concern in all this. She'd only ever been intended as a bonus in the transaction. His personal perquisite. He would simply be forced to write her off as a loss. Well—he was a businessman. He would understand that, and shrug.

And although she would be freed from any kind of sexual partnership with him, and ultimate and inevitable heartbreak, she would make sure she was nothing less than the perfect chatelaine for Monteagle. He would have no complaints about the way his home was run, or her behaviour as his hostess.

She sighed, and trailed across to the dressing room. In the meantime she'd have to pretend that this was the first day of a normal marriage and find something appropriate to wear.

Much as she might wish it, she could hardly go for the full covered-up blouse and skirt look when the temperature was clearly in the high eighties. Besides, Marc might even regard that as some kind of challenge, and that was the last thing she wanted.

It was probably better to attempt the role of radiant bride, she thought. And her pride demanded that she should behave as if the previous night had never happened, even if she was still weeping inside.

Eventually, as a concession to the climate, she picked out a black bikini that wasn't too indecently brief, topping it with its own filmy mid-thigh shirt.

But, in spite of her fears, it was only Elise who was waiting for her as she apprehensively descended the stairs half an hour later.

'*Bonjour, madame.*' Her eyes were twinkling. 'You 'ave sleep well, I think? Your 'usband say to let you rest as long as you desire. But now you like *un petit dejeuner*?'

'Just coffee, please,' Helen said, self-consciously aware that her watch was saying it was long past breakfast-time. She glanced around her. 'Er—where is *monsieur*?' she ventured.

''E 'as go for drive into the 'ills,' Elise informed her. 'But 'e will come back soon. For the lunch. It is my fish soup, which 'e does not miss.' She nodded with satisfaction, then bustled off to get the coffee.

Well, she was being allowed a brief respite at least, Helen thought. Given a breathing space to decide how she should behave and what she should actually say when she encountered him at last.

Elise's coffee was a dark and vibrant brew, and it managed to rid Helen's head of the last unhappy wisps of mental fog and enable her to think clearly.

It was vitally important not to give Marc the idea that she cared too much about the bleak conclusion to their wedding night.

Perhaps she should give the impression that it was no more than she'd expected. Or maybe she should wait, she thought. Judge his mood when he returned. Leave it to him to dictate the scenario.

In the meantime, this was a wonderful house, with beautiful grounds and the luxury of a swimming pool. At least she could allow herself a little enjoyment.

She finished her coffee, then set off. The pool was sited in a sunken area of the garden, surrounded by flower-filled shallow terraces. At the deep end of the azure water was a diving board, while a small hexagonal pavilion had been built at the opposite end for changing purposes, and to house a comprehensively equipped refrigerator.

Cushioned loungers, each with its own parasol, had been set round the surrounding tiled area.

Helen applied some high-factor sun lotion and lay down, sighing gratefully. There was a paperback book in her canvas bag, but, for a while anyway, she preferred to close her eyes and drift, blocking out the dark fears and uncertainties that plagued her, her head full, instead, of the distant wash of the sea and the busy hum of insects among the flowers.

She almost slept.

The sudden instinctive awareness that she was no longer alone brought her back to full consciousness, her eyes flying open to see Marc standing at the foot of the flight of shallow steps. He was wearing black swimming briefs, and, apart from the thin cotton shirt flung over one shoulder, the rest of him was tanned skin.

For one shocked, unguarded moment, she was pierced by a shaft of yearning so strong it seemed to penetrate her bones.

And he was looking at her too, his mouth unsmiling, his eyes masked by his sunglasses.

He said laconically, '*Ça va?*'

'Fine,' she said, jack-knifing herself into a sitting position too swiftly and defensively. It had suddenly occurred to her that apart from last night, this was the nearest to naked Marc had ever seen her, and the realisation made her feel disquieted and uncomfortable.

'I regret this intrusion,' he went on. 'But Elise was insistent that I needed a swim before lunch.' He tossed the shirt on to another lounger. 'She feels, I think, that I am neglecting my bride,' he added, his mouth twisting. 'I could hardly tell her that I am merely obeying your wishes.' He paused. 'Unless, of course, you would like to join me in the pool?'

Helen swallowed. 'Another time—perhaps.'

'Why pretend?' Marc asked derisively. 'Why not say no?'

She turned away. She said in a stifled voice, 'Isn't it a little late for that?'

'Perhaps that is something we should discuss.' He walked across and sat down on the end of her lounger. He'd discarded his sunglasses and his expression was searching—sombre. She watched him, her own eyes wary, her body tensing instinctively at his proximity.

She said, 'You mean to apologise—for last night?'

'Apologise?' His brows lifted. 'No. Let us say instead, *ma mie*, that neither of us was very kind—or very wise—in our treatment of each other, and put last night far behind us.'

'How can we do that?' Helen asked stiffly.

'By agreeing that it is the present—and our future together—that should concern us more.'

Her small workmanlike hands were gripped tightly together. 'What future is that?'

He sighed, his mouth tightening. 'I have taken you as my wife, Hélène. How can we live as strangers?'

She lifted her chin. 'Because that's what we are—as last night proved.'

'It proved nothing,' Marc said shortly. 'Except that you had decided for some reason that you no longer wanted me.'

'No longer?' Helen echoed indignantly. 'When did I ever?'

His brows rose sardonically. 'You wish me to list the times, perhaps?' There was a pause then he added, 'I regret that I did not seduce you when I had the chance, *ma belle*, instead of waiting to offer you the security of marriage first.'

'Perhaps,' Helen said stonily, hating the colour that had flared in her face at the unforgivable truth of his words, 'perhaps even then you wouldn't have found me as easy as you seem to believe.'

'I never expected to find you easy, Hélène,' he returned softly. 'Merely—infinitely rewarding.' He smiled faintly. 'As your beautiful mouth promises, *mon coeur*. The mouth you would not allow me to kiss last night in case you melted for me as your ancestress once did for the King,' he added quietly.

The breath seemed to catch in her throat. 'You—flatter yourself, *monsieur*,' she said. 'And you're quite wrong, too. They were different people in a different age. No comparison.'

He shrugged, his mouth wry, '*Bien sûr*, I am not a king, but a good republican—and I am your husband as well as your lover. But are we really so far apart? She fled him and he followed, just as I am here with you now, in spite of all that has happened.'

'We're a world away.' Her voice sounded thick and strained. 'And you are *not* my lover.'

For a moment his head went back as if she'd struck him, and he was silent.

'Then may we not begin again?' he asked at last, his voice deepening huskily. 'You are my wife, Hélène, and I want you—I long to show you how it should be between us. How it can be. If only…'

He reached for her hand, but she snatched it away.

'*Ah, Dieu.*' Marc shook his head. He was silent for a long moment, then said gently, 'Don't fight me any more, *cherie*. Let me come to you tonight and make love to you, as I wish to do. If you would only allow it, I know I could make you happy.'

'I think you're more concerned with your own satisfaction,' Helen flung at him. 'And the fact that your masculine pride's been damaged. In spite of your fantasies, last night can't have been particularly *rewarding* for you.'

'Or for you,' he said with sudden harshness.

It was her turn to shrug. 'Nevertheless,' she said, 'that's as good as it gets. Come to me—stay away—it makes no difference.'

She saw the dark eyes flare and his mouth harden.

He got to his feet in one lithe movement and stood over her, reminding her suddenly of the previous night, his body poised above hers. Forcing her to remember that piercing instant of need...

She went rigid, her eyes almost blank with fright, and saw his mouth move in a faint smile that was almost a sneer.

'Sois tranquille,' he said coldly. 'I shall not ask again.'

He turned away and walked to the edge of the pool. His body cut the water in a clean dive.

Heart hammering, she scrambled off the lounger, cramming on her shirt and picking up her pretty embroidered beach bag.

She went hurriedly up the steps, not looking behind her. Back to the house, she thought shakily. Out of harm's way.

Yet she knew at the same time that it was not that simple. *She fled him and he followed.* That was what Marc had said. And, in spite of that icy parting assurance from him, Helen knew she would never feel completely safe again while they were under the same roof.

She made herself go down to lunch when Elise came, clearly puzzled, to call her. For one thing she needed to repair the damage done by that moment of recoil at the pool. She'd shown Marc too clearly that he had the power to disturb her, and then, even more stupidly, she'd run away.

Also, more prosaically, she was hungry.

He was already waiting at the table that had been set for them in the shade of the terrace, and rose formally as she approached, his eyes skimming over the pale green sundress with its halter strap that she'd changed into, although he refrained from the comment she'd expected as she seated herself opposite him and unfolded her napkin.

He had changed too, she realised, into dark blue linen trousers and a matching polo shirt, and his still-damp hair was combed back from his face. As Elise arrived with the tureen he smiled up at her, said something teasing in his own language, and the force of his attraction made Helen catch her breath.

Concentrate on the food, she adjured herself silently. It's safer that way.

The fish soup was delicious, aromatic and filling, forcing her to eat sparingly of the platter of cold meats and salad that followed, and choose just a peach from the bowl of fresh fruit that ended the meal.

She declined any coffee, and was rising to her feet when he said crisply, '*Un moment, madame.*'

Helen halted, startled and reluctant.

'We need to reach a certain level of agreement.' Marc did not look at her as he filled his own cup. 'Whatever our private arrangements, we should try to behave in front of others as if we were truly *les nouveaux mariés. Par chance*, we do not have to stay here for very long, but we need to spend some time together each day—and in public.'

Helen bit her lip. 'Is that really necessary?'

'By now the news of our marriage will have reached the newspapers, and the gossip columnists will know we are here.' He shrugged. 'They will wish to take photographs of us together—being happy. We should indulge them. What happens at night is the business of no one but ourselves,' he added coldly.

Helen bit her lip. She said, 'I suppose—if we must. What—what do you suggest?'

'You overwhelm me.' His tone was barbed. 'To begin with, I propose we go down to St Benoit. The car and driver have been placed at our service, so I have ordered him to come round in half an hour. With Louis at the wheel, you do not even have to be alone with me.' He paused, allowing that to strike home. 'Also I intend to work for part of each day,' he went on. 'There are matters that require my attention even on honeymoon, so I recommend you use the pool area during those times, in case the sight of you in a bikini arouses me beyond bearing.'

Unhappy colour rose in her face. 'Please—don't talk like that.'

'Tes conditions sont trop rigoureuses, ma mie,' he told her mockingly. 'I cannot sleep with you—I may not even swim with you—and it is obvious you would prefer to eat alone. These I accept. But I refuse to censor my words—or my thoughts. *D'accord?'*

There was a silence, then Helen nodded jerkily. 'As you wish.'

'I recommend you treat your time with me like medicine, *cherie.'* Marc swallowed the remainder of his coffee and replaced the cup on its saucer. His eyes were hard. 'To be taken quickly and as soon forgotten.' He rose to his feet. 'Half an hour, then. And try, if you can, to smile for the cameras as if you were happy. This week will soon pass.'

By the time they came back to the villa that evening Helen had already reached at least one conclusion.

In the sunlit hours, she thought, she could—just—play the role assigned to her. But it would be an entirely different matter when the velvety darkness descended. That was altogether too intimate an ambience, and if she was to survive, as she must, her evenings had to be her own.

So when Marc turned to her after dinner and invited her to go with him to the Yacht Club, for coffee and brandies, she refused, saying mendaciously she had a headache.

'Pauvre petite.' His mouth curled with faint irony. 'Do you wish me to remain here and cherish you?'

'No, thank you,' she returned coolly. 'I'm not chained to your wrist. You're free to go out alone whenever you want.'

'How sweet you are,' he drawled mockingly. 'And how understanding.' He paused. 'I shall try not to disturb you on my return.'

Elise, who was clearing the table, sent them a look that said

louder than words that such a new wife should *expect* to be
disturbed by her husband, and should, *en effet*, actively welcome it, headache or not.

Marc walked over to Helen, dark and devastating in his tux-
edo, and bent, his lips swiftly brushing her hair.

He said quietly, 'Sleep well,' and went.

There was a silence, then Elise said dourly, 'I will fetch you
a powder, *madame*, for ze 'eadache.'

She not only fetched it, she stood over Helen while she swallowed the foul-tasting thing. 'Now you will be restored for the
return of *monsieur*,' she said with a firm nod.

But Helen wasn't so sure. The tension of walking round St
Benoit Plage all afternoon, hand in hand with Marc, was threat-
ening her with a genuine headache. It had been quite an ordeal
for her, however impersonal his touch.

The villa was equipped with a state-of-the-art audio system
and an eclectic mix of music. Helen curled up on one of the
giant hide sofas in the *salon* and put on some slow sweet jazz.
But the music alone couldn't stop her thinking, her mind re-
playing all the events of the past twenty-four hours. Above all
she found herself wondering what Marc was doing—and who
he might be with.

She'd been aware all afternoon of the predatory glances being aimed at him by tanned and sexy women keen to get closer
regardless of her presence. And now she'd turned him out on
the town alone…

But then what choice did she have? she argued defensively
with herself. She certainly had no right to expect physical fi-
delity from him.

Sighing, she picked up one of the glossy magazines arranged
on the low table in front of her and began to flick over the
pages. She paused to glance at a double-page spread showing
people attending a charity performance at the opera. The name
'Angeline Vallon' seemed to leap out at her.

She looked at the accompanying picture, her heart beating
slowly and unevenly.

She saw a tall, beautiful woman, with a mane of dark auburn
hair tumbling down her back, standing beside a much smaller

man with a beard and a faintly peevish expression, described as 'her industrialist husband Hercule'.

Madame Vallon was wearing a very low-cut evening gown that set off her frankly voluptuous body, and a magnificent diamond necklace circled her throat.

She didn't look like someone who had to ask more than once for what she wanted, thought Helen, trying not to wince. Nor someone who would be easily persuaded to let go.

And you're quite right to opt for self-preservation, she told herself stoically. Because you're no competition for her. No competition at all.

She closed the magazine, replacing it with meticulous ex-actitude on the table, and made her solitary way up to bed.

But not to sleep. Not until much later, when she eventually heard quiet footsteps passing her room, without breaking stride even for a moment, and then the sound of Marc's door closing.

Helen turned on to her stomach, pressing her burning face into the pillow.

I shall not ask again. That, after all, was what he'd told her. And apparently he'd meant every word.

Somehow she had to be grateful for this one mercy at least.

But, dear God, how painfully, grindingly difficult that was going to be for her. And she found herself stifling a sob.

CHAPTER TEN

MARC had told her the time would pass quickly, but to Helen the days that followed seemed more like an eternity. Yet under other circumstances she knew they could have been wonderful.

From that first afternoon in St Benoit Plage she seemed to have stepped through the looking glass into a different and totally unreal world, peopled only by the beautiful and the seriously affluent.

To her astonishment, Marc had been right about the photographers, and Helen had been chagrined to find herself described in the local news sheet as 'charming but shy', under a picture of her with her mouth open, clinging to her husband's hand as if he was her last hope of salvation.

Not shy, she'd thought wryly. Just shocked witless at all this unwonted attention.

'Relax, *ma mie*,' Marc had advised, clearly amused. 'They will soon focus on someone else.'

In the days that followed he took her to Cannes, Nice and Monte Carlo, until her mind was a blur of smart restaurants and glamorous shops. She had learned early on not to linger outside the windows of boutiques, or admire anything too openly, otherwise the next moment Marc would have bought it for her. It was heady stuff for someone who'd existed up to now on a skeleton wardrobe, but she found his casual generosity disturbing.

No doubt he treated his mistresses equally lavishly, she thought unhappily, but at least they deserved it. Whereas she, patently, did not.

Not that he cared, she told herself defensively. After all, when this pathetic honeymoon had stumbled to its close he had Angeline Vallon waiting for him. And life would return to normal for them both.

She had to admit that Marc had kept his word about their own relationship. He'd made sure from the first that they were rarely alone together. In the car, with Louis as unwitting chaperone, they exchanged polite but stilted conversation, and at the villa, as he'd suggested, they pursued a policy of positive avoidance, under the frankly disapproving gaze of Gaston and Elise, who were clearly baffled by these strange newlyweds.

She had no idea where or how Marc spent his evenings, although she was always courteously invited to accompany him and had to struggle to invent excuses. She only knew that she lay sleepless, listening for his return, however late it happened to be. And how sad was that?

There were times when she longed to confront him—tell him to his face that she knew he had a mistress. But that would only betray to him how much it mattered to her, and she couldn't risk that. Couldn't admit that he had the power to hurt her.

Also, he might ask how she knew. And she could hardly confess that she'd been eavesdropping.

It was far less humiliating to simply keep quiet and count her blessings that she still had Monteagle, if nothing else.

She halted, startled, aware that she'd never regarded the situation in that light before. Always her home had been paramount in her thoughts. She'd said openly that she would do anything to save it, yet now, for the first time, she was counting the cost and finding it oddly bitter.

It will be easier when I go home, she promised herself. When I get back to the real world again.

And yet, as she at last began packing for the return journey, she found herself feeling oddly wistful—even empty. And for once she had a genuine headache. The sky had become overcast towards the end of the afternoon, and she wasn't surprised to hear a faint rumble of thunder from the hills.

When she arrived downstairs for dinner, she found that Gaston had prudently laid the table in the *salle à manger* instead of the terrace. 'It makes to rain, *madame*,' he told her lugubriously.

Elise came bustling in with a dish of home-made duck pâté.

'*Monsieur* begs you will commence,' she announced. ''E is engaged with the telephone.'

It was over ten minutes later when Marc eventually made his unsmiling appearance. 'I regret that I have kept you waiting.' The apology sounded cursory, and he ate his meal almost in silence, his thoughts quite evidently elsewhere.

Eventually, when coffee was served and they were alone, he said abruptly, 'We will be leaving for the airport in the morning, *à dix heures*. Can you be ready?'

Helen put down her cup. 'Has the flight been changed?'

'We are not catching the London plane,' he said. 'We shall be spending a short time in Paris instead.'

'Paris?' she echoed. 'But where will we stay?'

'I once told you that I have an *appartement* there,' he said.

'Yes,' she said. 'And a hotel suite in London.'

His faint smile was twisted. 'The *appartement* is larger, *je t'assure*. To begin with, there is more than one bedroom,' he added pointedly.

She flushed dully, annoyed that he should read her so accurately. 'All the same,' she said stiffly, 'I'd prefer to go straight home.'

He glanced at her meditatively. 'You are my wife, Hélène,' he said quietly. 'It might be thought that wherever I am your home is with me.'

'We don't have that kind of marriage.' She didn't look at him. 'And, anyway, I need to be at Monteagle. I want to see what progress has been made there. Besides, what would I do in Paris—apart from cramp your style?' she added recklessly.

Marc's brows lifted. 'Cramp my style?' he queried, as if he'd never heard the phrase before. 'In what way, may I ask?'

Helen bit her lip. 'Well—you have things to do—people to see,' she offered nervously, backing away from his challenge. 'And I'd be in the way.' She poured herself some more coffee. 'Anyway, I think we both need—breathing space—from each other.'

'You think so?' His tone was mocking. 'Shall I calculate for you, *cherie*, exactly how many hours we have spent together this week? Not that it matters, of course. Monteagle calls, and you obey.' He paused. 'So, I will go to Paris alone, and arrange to have you met at the airport in England.'

He swallowed the rest of his coffee and rose. 'And now you will excuse me. I intend to try my luck at the casino again tonight.'

'Is that where you've been spending your evenings?' Helen asked the question before she could stop herself. 'I didn't realise you were such a gambler.'

'And nor did I, *ma belle*,' Marc said softly, 'until I met you. And I find the turn of a wheel or the fall of a card infinitely kinder, believe me.' He kissed the tips of his fingers to her. *'Au revoir.'*

Helen hated thunderstorms. But she was almost grateful to this one for giving her something more to worry about than her immediate problems. After all, she'd won a victory over her return to Monteagle, she thought defensively. So why did it feel so much like a defeat? And Marc's absence so soon after the honeymoon would excite the kind of local comment she most wished to avoid.

But anything was better than accompanying him to Paris, like a piece of extra luggage.

And he certainly hadn't tried too hard to persuade her, either, Helen told herself defiantly.

She spent a restless evening trying to read, while lightning played around the hills, making the villa's electricity flicker. Eventually she gave it up as a bad job and went to bed.

Perhaps it was the prospect of going home that made her feel more relaxed, but tonight she found herself drifting into a doze almost at once.

When she awoke, everything was pitch-black and completely silent. The storm, it seemed, had rolled away at last, leaving the room like an oven and the bedclothes twisted round her. Clearly she hadn't been sleeping as peacefully as she'd thought. She struggled out of the shrouding covers and got out of bed, treading across to the window and opening it wide to step out on to the balcony, planning to cool off a little.

But the air outside was just as stifling. Helen leaned on the balustrade and inhaled, but the garden smelled raw and thirsty, and possessed by a strange stillness, as if it was waiting in anticipation of—what?

A moment later she found out. As if some cosmic tap had been turned, the rain began to fall in huge, soaking drops, and by the time Helen made it back into her room she was already wet through, her nightgown sticking in clammy dampness to her skin.

Grimacing, she peeled it off and dropped it to the floor. She discarded the coverlet from the bed, too, and slid back under the single sheet, listening to the heavy splash of rain on the balcony tiles, hoping it would have a soporific effect.

She had to train herself not to lie awake listening for Marc, she told herself wearily, because there would be so many nights when he would not be there. Starting with tomorrow.

She turned on to her side, facing the window, and stiffened as a tall shadow walked in from the balcony and moved soundlessly towards her. She wanted to scream, but her throat muscles didn't seem to be working.

Then the heavily shaded lamp at the side of the bed clicked on, and she realised it was Marc, his hair hanging in damp tendrils, water glistening on his dinner jacket.

She said hoarsely, 'What are you doing here?'

'I came to tell you that I won tonight.' He reached into his pocket and took out a packet of high denomination euros. 'Every table I sat at yielded gold.'

'I'm very pleased for you,' Helen said tautly. 'But the morning would have done for your news.'

He smiled down at her. His black tie was hanging loose, and several of the buttons on his dress shirt were unfastened. 'But it is the morning, *ma mie*. And besides, I have something else I wish to share with you.'

'Can't it wait?' She tried unobtrusively to raise the sheet to chin level. 'I—I'm very tired.'

'And I,' he said, 'have waited long enough. On our wedding night you accused me of buying you for sex. If so, Hélène, I made a poor bargain. And it occurred to me, as I came back tonight, that perhaps I had not yet paid enough for the privilege of enjoying your charming body. So—'

He scattered some of the banknotes across the bed. 'How much will this buy me, *mon coeur*? A smile—a kiss, *peut-être*? Or even—this.'

He reached down and took the edge of the sheet from her, stripping it back to the foot of the bed, leaving her naked.

'Oh, God,' Helen said, with a little wail of shock. She tried to curl into the foetal position, covering what she could of herself with her shaking hands. 'You said—' she accused breathlessly. 'You told me you wouldn't ask again.'

'But I am not asking,' he said gently. 'This time I am taking.'

'But why?' There was a sob in her voice. 'Weren't there any women at the casino you could have chosen—with all that money?'

'Dozens,' Marc told her pleasantly. 'And all of them more eager and welcoming than you, *ma chère*. But I decided I preferred a little—domestic entertainment.' He paused. 'And you can always close your eyes—pretend that I am someone else.'

Quietly ruthless, he unpeeled her arms from her body, one hand closing on both her slender wrists and lifting them above her head. Holding them there. Helen cried out in startled protest as his other hand grasped her ankles, straightening her body and drawing it gently but inexorably down the bed, leaving her with nowhere to hide from the insolent hunger in his dark gaze.

'Marc,' she whispered imploringly. 'I beg you—please don't do this.'

Marc lifted himself on to the bed and knelt over her, trapping her legs between his knees while he studied her.

He said quietly, '*Tu es vraiment exquise, Hélène*. And this is what your body was made for.' Then he bent his head and began to kiss her, his lips cool as the rain as they touched her.

Helen tried to resist, her mouth clamped shut, her head twisting frantically on the pillow. But he was not to be denied.

His tongue was like a flame against hers, teasing her slowly and sensuously, demanding that her lips yield him their innermost secrets. At the same time his hand found one small, pointed breast, his fingertips delicately stroking its soft curve, wringing a response that urged the nipple to bloom sweetly and helplessly into his caressing palm.

Helen found herself almost unable to breathe—to think. He was still clasping her wrists—but so loosely that she could have pulled free at any time, at least tried to fight him off. Instead, she realised she was sighing into his mouth, her body gradually slackening under the sensuous insistence of his lips and fingers.

When he had finished with her she would die of shame at her own weakness, she told herself dazedly. But for now...

His mouth moved down to her throat, making the pulse there leap and flutter. He explored the soft hollows at its base, then trailed kisses down to her breasts, his lips suckling each excited peak in turn, piercing them with sensations she'd never dreamed of.

When at last he raised his head she stared up at him, her eyes wide with bewilderment, her lips slightly parted.

He touched them lightly with his own, then released her wrists, turning her slightly so that the long, supple line of her back was at the mercy of his mouth instead, while his hands still stroked and pleasured her tumescent breasts.

He brushed the soft strands of hair away from the nape of her neck with his mouth, and she felt her whole body quiver in helpless response to the caress.

His lips and tongue travelled slowly, almost languidly, between her shoulderblades and down her spine, as if he was counting each delicate bone with kisses, while his fingers pursued their own erotic path across her ribcage to the flat plane of her stomach, coming to rest on the slender curves of her hipbones.

As he caressed the sensitive area at the base of her spine she gave a muffled moan and her body arched involuntarily, vulnerably. He drew her back against him, his arm across her breasts. At the same moment his other hand moved, cupping the soft mound at the parting of her slackened thighs with terrifying intimacy.

'No—please.' Helen's voice splintered as his fingertips began their first silken journey of discovery into the moist, scalding heat of her most secret self.

Marc kissed the side of her throat and she felt him smile against her skin. 'No?'

His hand moved, delicately, subtly, and she cried out, her body writhing helplessly against his enfolding arm.

Suddenly, unexpectedly, he turned her on to her back, and she caught a dazed glimpse of the heated glitter in his eyes. But she had no idea of his real purpose as he bent to her, his hands sliding under her flanks, lifting her towards him. The next instant, before she could move to prevent him, his mouth had taken possession of her, and the powerful glide of his tongue had sought and found the tiny hidden bud, continuing its exquisite arousal.

Helen's entire being tensed in shock, followed immediately by an agony of guilty, terrified delight. She tried once more to say no. To find the strength, somehow, to push him away and stop this shameful, delicious pleasure before it carried her away beyond all the barriers she'd tried to build against him.

But the only sound that came from her throat was a small sob. She closed her eyes in a desperate attempt to distance herself—to hang on to some kind of self-control. But it was already too late.

Her awareness had shrunk to the distant splash of the rain, her own jagged, fevered breathing, and the hot, beautiful semi-darkness that surrounded her—invaded her. She knew nothing but the response that Marc was forcing from her trembling body, the alchemy of his experienced caresses, seducing her bewildered senses and sweeping away her innocence for ever.

The pleasure began slowly, at first little more than a breeze rippling across still water, then building with irresistible, quivering urgency into a great wave, gathering force and speed as it lifted her, all control gone, to some unimagined peak of rapture and held her there.

Then the wave broke, and she crashed with it, helpless, whimpering, torn apart by the spasms of ecstasy that possessed her.

She lay dazed and trembling, unable to speak or move, or

even to comprehend what had just happened to her. She was no longer certain where she was, or even who she was.

A strange euphoria was spreading throughout her body. Every bone, muscle and skin cell was utterly relaxed, tingling with this new delight, as if she was floating in some beatific dream, drained and weightless.

She was dimly aware that Marc had moved away from her, and found herself reaching out a bereft hand, searching for him blindly across the empty bed.

'*Sois tranquille, mon amour.* I am here.' His voice was a whisper. He'd used his brief absence to strip, she realised, as he drew her to him, and she gasped silently as she felt the warmth of his aroused and powerful nakedness against her body.

Instinctively, she arched towards him, thrilling again at his touch, her arms circling his neck, the tips of her breasts grazing his hair-roughened chest, and heard him groan softly. His hands took her gently, positioning her, then he entered her with one strong, fluid thrust.

Her yielding was total, immediate. Almost languidly she lifted her legs, locking them round his hips, her own movements mirroring the smooth, almost voluptuous drive of his loins, drawing him deeper still into her body.

'Tell me.' His voice was a hoarse whisper. 'Tell me if I hurt you.'

'I want you.' Her reply was hardly more than a breath. 'I want—everything…'

She'd thought after that previous implosion of ecstasy that still lingered, suffusing her with its joy, she would find herself exhausted, emptied of sensation, incapable of anything but compliance. But she was wrong.

The controlled force of his possession was evoking a response that went far beyond mere surrender. Suddenly her body was coming unexpectedly, ardently to life again, and as his rhythm increased, became fiercer, she found she was being carried away with him, striving with him on some long, sweet spiral of such intensity that it frightened her.

Pleasure hovered on the verge of pain, and she heard herself crying out, crushing her mouth against his shoulder as the long, shuddering convulsions of her climax pulled her over the edge into Paradise. Seconds later he followed her, wildly groaning her name as he reached the white heat of fulfilment in his turn.

Afterwards they lay quietly in a tangle of sweat-soaked limbs, his arms holding her as she pillowed her head on his chest, both waiting for the storm of their breathing to subside.

But for Helen the descent to earth was swift, and soon unhappy.

Because now she knew there was no more room for pretence. She had taken as completely as she had given. And by so doing she'd sacrificed her self-respect, and any forlorn hope of feigning her indifference.

However it might have begun, Marc had given her a night she would remember always. But soon he would be lying with his lips against someone else's hair, his long fingers drowsily caressing another woman's breast. And she'd allowed herself to forget that for the sake of a few hours of total ravishment.

A little domestic entertainment. The coolly jeering words came back to haunt her. Because that was all he wanted—to ensure that when he came to Monteagle she'd be waiting for him with passionate eagerness, ready to give him anything he wanted. A perpetual honeymoon, Helen thought, biting her lower lip, still swollen from his kisses. Until, of course, her sexual education was complete, by which time her novelty for him would probably have worn off.

And all this pain—this heartbreak—she had brought upon herself.

I shall have to learn not to think, she told herself, as Marc's soft, regular breathing informed her that he'd fallen asleep. Not to wonder what he's doing when he's away, or who he might be with. No scenes and no accusations.

If I can manage to turn a perpetually blind eye, and he is reasonably discreet, then maybe our separate lives can be made to work.

She leaned across and switched off the lamp.

And now, she thought, she would try to sleep.

*   *   *

She opened her eyes to sunshine and birdsong, and Marc bending over her, clearly about to kiss her—and not for the first time, she thought, blushing, assailed by a vivid memory of him kissing her awake in the early dawn, and making love to her with such tenderness and grace that afterwards she'd found herself weeping in his arms.

'*Bonjour.*' He propped himself on an elbow and smiled at her. 'You awaken very beautifully.'

Her blush deepened. At some point during the night he must have retrieved the sheet, she realised, and covered her with it, because she now had a shield against the over-bright light of day. And, more importantly, against his eyes.

'Good morning,' she said, a touch awkwardly. 'Has—has the rain stopped?'

'You are a true Englishwoman, *cherie*.' He was laughing. 'You wish to discuss the weather even when you are in bed with your lover.'

But you're not my lover, she thought with sudden pain, even as her body clenched once more in unwilling yearning. Last night had nothing to do with love. It was simply a vindication of your own prowess in bed, because I rejected you. You needed to prove that you could make me want you against my own will and judgement. And against all reason—because I'm not the only woman in your life, and we both know it.

'I'm sorry,' she said stiffly.

'No, you must not be. It is charming.' He leaned down and kissed her mouth softly. 'And I wish very much that we could stay here for ever, but we have a plane to catch. Besides,' he added, stroking her cheek, 'there will be tonight.'

'Two planes,' Helen corrected, remembering the resolution she'd made last night and how badly she needed to keep it. He only had to look at her, she thought. Or smile. Or touch her lightly with a fingertip, and she was dying to melt in his arms. But she could not allow him to do this to her. Could not—would not—live this lie with him. 'We—we're on different flights.' She took a steadying breath. 'And yours, if you remember, is the earliest.'

'Different flights?' Marc repeated slowly. 'What are you

talking about? We will be travelling together. You are coming with me to Paris, *naturellement*.'

'No,' she said. 'I'm going back to England and Monteagle, as we agreed.'

Marc sat up abruptly, the sheet falling away from his body, and she looked away swiftly. Oh, God, she needed no reminders...

He said, 'But that was yesterday—before...'

'Before we had sex, you mean? You feel that should make some difference?' She kept her voice light. 'I don't see why.'

'I had hoped,' he said very quietly, 'that perhaps you would want to be with me. Now that we have found each other at last.'

But not in Paris, she wanted to scream at him. Never in Paris—at this famous apartment of yours, in the bed where you make love to your mistress. Don't you see that I *can't* go there? And that I won't—ever?

'But I shall be with you,' she returned instead. 'That is whenever you choose to come back to Monteagle.'

'Which may not be for some time,' he said. He looked at her steadily. 'That does not concern you?'

'You may come and go as you please. It's not up to me to interfere in your life—your decisions.' The rawness in her heart gave her voice an edge.

'I believed,' he said with sudden bleakness, 'that I had given you that right. So why do you refuse me?' He paused, and his voice hardened. 'Is it because there is some other one involved in our relationship? Has that come between us? Answer me.'

'You seem to know already.' She felt her heart give a sudden jolt. She hadn't intended this, she thought wretchedly. She hadn't thought he'd want to discuss Angeline Vallon or any of his women with her. She'd assumed he'd prefer her to ignore the rumours which would no doubt reach her. That he'd expect gratitude for Monteagle to keep her silent.

Why, she asked herself desperately, wasn't he playing according to the rules? But then, when had Marc ever done so?

'*Ah, Mon Dieu.*' He almost groaned the words, then was silent for a moment. At last, he said unevenly, 'Hélène—you are being a fool. Yet in spite of all this we can make our marriage work—I know it. This—other thing—it will not last. It cannot. And you cannot allow it to matter. To damage what we might have together.

'*Cherie.*' His voice deepened. 'You must not do this to yourself—to us.'

Us, Helen thought. There is no 'us' and never can be. Because even when Angeline Vallon is history, as you suggest, there'll be someone else in her place. There'll always be someone else—for a month or two...

'But I can't pretend it doesn't exist either,' she said raggedly. 'That wasn't part of the deal. So I shan't be going with you to Paris.' She took a deep breath. 'But Monteagle is yours too, of course, and when you choose to be there I'm prepared to reach some—compromise with you.'

'As you did last night?' The words slammed at her.

'Yes,' she said defiantly. 'Exactly like that.'

He said something under his breath—something harsh and ugly—then threw himself off the bed, grabbing for his discarded clothing. But he made no attempt to dress himself.

Instead, he reached into the pocket of his dinner jacket. 'Then allow me to congratulate you on your performance, *madame.*' His voice seared her like acid. 'You learn quickly—and, as I explained, I would not wish you to go unrewarded for your efforts.'

He tossed the roll of money into the air, and watched the banknotes flutter down on to the bed around her.

'Consider yourself paid in full, *ma femme,*' he added. 'Until the next time—wherever and whenever that may be.'

And he left her, white-faced and stricken, staring after him, as he strode to the door and vanished.

CHAPTER ELEVEN

'YOU mean it?' Lottie's face lit up. 'You'll let me have my wedding reception in the Long Gallery? Oh, Helen, that's wonderful.'

Helen returned her hug. 'Well, you can't squeeze everyone into your cottage—not without appalling casualties and structural damage anyway,' she added drily. 'And the Gallery looks terrific now it's finished. It really needs to be used for something special.'

Lottie hesitated. 'And you're sure Marc won't mind?'

'Why should he?' Helen asked with a light shrug. *As he's so rarely here…* She thought it, but did not say it aloud.

'I only wanted a tiny wedding,' Lottie said mournfully. 'A few close friends and family.' She sighed. 'But that was before our respective mothers presented us with their final guest lists, and a string of other instructions as well. I've had to rethink all my catering plans, for one thing, as well as dashing off to the wedding hire place in Aldenford for some ghastly meringue and veil.'

Helen patted her consolingly. 'You'll look wonderful,' she said. 'And I guarantee Simon will be secretly thrilled.' She paused. 'Shall we get some music laid on for dancing? Really test the Gallery's new floor?'

'Why not?' Her friend shrugged lavishly. 'In for a penny, in for a pound. The whole nine yards.' She gave Helen a speculative glance. 'Does Marc like dancing? I mean, he will make it to the wedding, I hope? Or will he be in Bolivia or Uzbekistan?'

'I—really don't know,' Helen admitted uncomfortably. 'But, wherever he is, I'm sure he'll do his best. I'll ask Alan to remind him. After all, he seems to see much more of him than I do,' she added, with attempted nonchalance.

159

There was another silence, then Lottie said fiercely, 'Oh, this is all so wrong—such a mess. Simon and I are so happy—so crazy about each other—and you're so damned miserable. And don't argue with me,' she warned, as Helen's lips parted in protest. 'Even a blind person could see it.'

'I have what I asked for,' Helen said quietly. 'And so has Marc.' She tried to smile. 'He seems quite content—and you have to admit the house is looking terrific.'

'I don't have to admit anything.' Lottie picked up her bag and prepared for departure. 'In fact there are times when I wish you'd sold Monteagle lock, stock and barrel to bloody Trevor Newson. So there.'

And there are times when I wish that too, Helen thought with sudden wry bitterness. The shocked breath caught in her throat as she realised what she had just admitted to herself.

She managed to keep a smile in place as she waved her friend off, but her stomach was churning and her legs felt oddly weak.

How can I suddenly feel like this? she asked herself as she made herself turn, walk back into the house she loved. The home she'd always considered worth any sacrifice.

Monteagle's been my life all this time. My lodestar. And so it should be still—because I have nothing else. Nothing...

She found she was making her way up the stairs, breathing the smell of paint, plaster and wood as she'd done for so many weeks. But, as usual, she encountered no one. The restoration team were busy at the other end of the house, and she was able to enter the State Bedroom once again unnoticed. Where she paused, staring round her, drinking in the room's completed beauty. And its strange emptiness.

The embroidery from the old bed curtains had been transferred exquisitely to its rich new fabric, and it gleamed in the mellow sunlight that poured in through the mullioned windows. While above the fireplace the other Helen Frayne looked enigmatically down on her descendant.

And, dominating the room, that enormous bed—made up each week with fresh linen, yet still unused.

Helen had stood in this room grieving after her grandfather's funeral, knowing that she was entirely alone. She'd tried with a kind of desperation to convince herself that it wasn't true. That she would spend her future with Nigel and find happiness and fulfilment—but only if she could save her beloved home and live there. That had always been the proviso.

No guy stands a chance against a no-win obsession like that. She found herself remembering Nigel's petulant accusation.

But it wasn't an obsession, she cried inwardly. It was a dream—wasn't it? Only now the dream was dead, and she didn't know why.

Except that she was lying to herself. Because it had begun to fade six weeks ago, when she came back from France.

Without Marc. Without even saying goodbye to Marc. Because he'd already left for the airport when she arrived downstairs that last morning at the Villa Mirage.

Later, on her own homeward journey, she'd asked Louis to stop at a little church she'd seen on the way out of St Benoit Plage, and she had filled the poor box to bursting with the euro notes that Marc had scattered so scornfully across her shocked body, hoping that by doing so she could somehow exorcise the stunned misery that was choking her.

All the way back to Monteagle she'd told herself over and over again that it would all be worth it once she was home. That somehow she'd even be able to survive this agony of bewildered loneliness once she could see her beautiful house coming back to life.

Only it hadn't been like that. Not when she'd realised that she was actually expected to move into this room—that bed—alone, and had known that she couldn't do it. That it was impossible. Unthinkable.

An unbearable solitude—worse than any imagining.

So she'd informed Daisy quietly that she'd prefer to sleep in her own bedroom for the time being, and the housekeeper, noting her pale face and tearless eyes, had tactfully not argued with her.

And there the matter rested. In distance and estrangement.

She'd explained, charmingly and ruefully, to anyone who asked that Marc was in serial business meetings and would join her as soon as he was free. But it was an excuse that sounded increasingly thin as a week had passed and edged into a fortnight without a word from him.

She'd found this lack of communication unnerving, and eventually swallowed her pride and approached Alan Graham.

'I was expecting Marc here this weekend,' she had fibbed, fingers crossed in the pockets of her skirt. 'But I've heard nothing—and I've stupidly mislaid his contact number in Paris. Do you know what's happening?'

'I certainly know that he's not in Paris,' Alan returned with a touch of dryness. 'He left for Botswana several days ago, and is going on to Senegal. He's unlikely to be back in Europe until next week, but even then I don't think he has any immediate plans to visit the UK.'

'I see.' Another lie. She forced a smile, but the architect's face remained impassive. 'Well, perhaps his secretary could supply me with a copy of his itinerary—or let me know if there's an opening in his schedule.'

She expected him to offer an address, a telephone extension and a name, but he did none of those things.

He hesitated perceptibly. 'Marc is incredibly busy, Mrs Delaroche. It might be better to leave it to him to get in touch—don't you think?'

In other words, if Marc had wanted her to make the first contact he'd have supplied her with the means, she realised, mortified. And Alan Graham—not just her husband's friend, but also his employee—had been instructed to block her, to keep her at a safe distance where she could not interfere with the way he lived his life.

'Yes,' she said, her voice stumbling over the word. 'Of course.'

As she turned to leave she saw an odd expression flicker in his eyes—something, she thought, which might have been pity. And her humiliation was complete.

Even now she could remember how she'd gone out of the house and walked round the lake, struggling to come to terms with the fact that her marriage was already virtually over.

Yes, she'd made him angry that last morning. But she'd been

upset, and desperately hurt. So how could he behave as if he was the only injured party in all this? If he cared for her at all, wouldn't he have been concerned more for her feelings and less for his own convenience?

Suggesting she should accompany him to Paris had been an act of brutal cynicism. Surely he must have realised that admitting there was another woman in his life had robbed her of any chance of peace and happiness whenever he was away from her?

Even now, when they were miles apart, she was still racked by jealousy and wretchedness. That last passionate, overwhelming night in France had done its work too well, creating a hunger that only he could assuage. But she was no longer a priority on his agenda.

She'd turned and stared at the bulk of the house through eyes blurred with tears. Her kingdom, she'd thought, where she ruled alone, just as she'd wanted. Her kingdom and her prison.

But even if Marc didn't want her, his plans for the house were clearly still foremost in his mind.

His team of craftsmen were still working flat out, over long hours, and she could only guess at the size of the wage bill being incurred. Also, the extra staff he'd insisted on were now in place—pleasant, efficient, and taking the pressure from George and Daisy. Far from feeling resentful, they were now talking cheerfully about the prospect of retirement on the pension that Marc had also set up for them.

'But what would I do without you?' Helen had asked, startled and distressed. 'I rely on you both totally. You're my family.'

Daisy had patted her gently. 'Everything changes, my dear. And you'll be having a new family soon—a proper one, with Monsieur Marc.'

Which, thought Helen, was almost a sick joke—under the circumstances.

She'd tried to keep busy, to stop herself from thinking, but apart from arranging the flowers and deciding what food to eat, there was little to occupy her at Monteagle, she had to admit. The place seemed to run like clockwork. Instead, she spent two days a week helping in a charity shop in Aldenford, and another afternoon pushing round the library trolley at the local cottage hospital.

So she'd been out when the longed-for telephone call had come to say Marc would be arriving the next day.

But her initial relief and elation had been dealt an immediate blow when Alan had informed her with faint awkwardness that this was simply a flying visit, to check on the progress of the house, and that Marc would be leaving again after lunch.

She'd managed a word of quiet assent, then taken herself up to her room, where she'd collapsed across the bed, weeping uncontrollably.

The next day she had departed early for a ceramics auction in a town twenty miles away. It had been purely a face-saving move. She had no particular interest in porcelain and pottery, and no intention of bidding on any of the lots.

She'd arrived back at Monteagle just before lunch was served, and returned Marc's cold greeting with equal reserve before eating her way through salmon mayonnaise and summer pudding as if she had an appetite, while Marc and Alan chatted together in French.

The meal over, she had been about to excuse herself when Marc detained her with an imperative gesture. Alan quietly left them alone together, standing on opposite sides of the dining table.

'The new staff? You find them acceptable?' he'd asked abruptly.

'Perfectly, thank you.' She hesitated. 'Of course it helps that they're local people.'

'And the house? The work continues to your satisfaction?'

'It all looks wonderful,' she said quietly. 'But naturally I shall be glad when it's over.'

There was an odd silence before he said, 'Then I hope for your sake, Hélène, that they continue to make the same progress and you are soon left in peace from all of this.' His brief smile did not reach his eyes. *'Au revoir,'* he added, and was gone.

And that, Helen thought unhappily, had set the pattern for

his two subsequent visits—except that Alan's wife had been invited to join them for lunch. But, as Susan treated her with the same polite aloofness as her husband, it couldn't be described as the most successful social experiment of the year.

There had never been any hint that he wished to spend the night here. In fact he didn't even want to touch her, she admitted, swallowing a desolate lump in her throat. It seemed that the beautiful Angeline was supplying all his needs, and that she herself was excluded from any intimate role in his life, however temporary.

Why did he do it? she asked herself. Why did he take me and make me want him so desperately that every day and night without him makes me feel as if I'm slowly bleeding to death?

But she already knew the answer. Because he could, she thought. And how cruel was that?

As unkind as the way he'd suddenly ended that brief interlude on the bed over there, she reminded herself. Her whole body had been singing to the touch of his mouth and hands when he'd stepped back, apparently unaffected by her response—except to be amused by it.

How silly and futile all her subsequent protests must have seemed to him—and how easily they'd been overcome, she thought bitterly. And she knew still that, in spite of everything, if he so much as beckoned to her she would go to him.

Her body was aching—starving for him. Demanding the surcease that only he could give, but which he chose to deny her.

Making it clear that there was no place for her even on the margins of his life.

Perhaps, she thought, wincing painfully, Angeline Vallon doesn't like sharing either, and has enough power to issue an ultimatum.

Sighing, she walked over to the portrait and stood staring up at it.

'How did you cope?' she asked softly. 'When your royal victor became tired of his spoils and moved on? How many days before you stopped hoping? How many long nights before he ceased to feature in your dreams? And what else must I endure before my sentence is served and I can get out of jail?'

On the other hand, if she did escape somehow, then where would she go?

Her mouth twisted wrily. Bolivia, she thought. Uzbekistan— or any of the places that Marc had been flying between over these long weeks. She'd always secretly yearned to travel, to get to the heart of cities and countries that were only names in an atlas, but she'd given up all hope of that for the sake of Monteagle.

If she could turn back time, she knew now she would have followed Marc downstairs that last morning, held out her hand and said, Take me with you. Because half a life at his side would have been better than no life at all.

A fly had appeared from nowhere, and was grumbling vainly against one of the windows. Helen walked across the room and opened the casement to allow it to escape, and stood suddenly transfixed, staring across the lawns below.

A woman was standing, a hand shading her eyes as she looked up at the house, her long red hair gleaming in the late summer sunlight.

No, Helen thought with disbelief. And, as the anger began to build in her, *No*.

Has Marc allowed this? she asked herself. Has he dared to let her invade my territory? And is she going to spend time here—with him—forcing me to move out for the duration? Why else would she be here, spying out the land?

Oh, God, she thought. How could he hurt me—insult me— like this?

She closed the casement with a bang and ran from the room, and down the stairs, almost flinging herself out into the open air.

As she reached the grass she saw the other woman walking rapidly towards the side gate.

She is not getting away with this, Helen told herself grimly. She'll stand her ground and hear what I have to say.

'Wait!' she called, cupping her hands round her mouth. *'Attendez, madame!'*

The other woman paused, turning as if surprised, then waited awkwardly, hands thrust into the pockets of her cream linen trousers, as Helen came running towards her.

She only stopped, breathless and shocked, when she realised that, apart from hair colour, her quarry bore no resemblance at all to the woman whose magazine picture still haunted her mercilessly.

She was considerably older, and thinner, and her face was pleasant rather than beautiful—although at the moment she looked embarrassed and wary.

'I'm sorry,' she said. 'The house isn't open to the public any more, is it? And I'm trespassing.'

'Yes, I'm afraid so.' Helen struggled to control her breathing. 'Did you want anything in particular?'

'Not really.' The other woman shrugged. 'Just a final glimpse, really. I went round with the guided tour a few times before the restoration work started, and I was curious to see if much had changed.'

Helen stared at her. 'You're quite a devotee.'

'I feel I've known the place all my life. You see, my great-grandmother was in service here years ago, and my grandmother too, and they loved it. I grew up with all these stories about Monteagle—felt as if I was part of them. Daft, I know, but we all have our dreams.'

She paused. 'You're Helen Frayne, aren't you? But you confused me when you called out in French. I thought that was your husband's nationality.'

'It is. I—I thought you were someone completely different. I'm sorry.' Helen hesitated. 'May I know who you really are?'

'Why not?' Another almost fatalistic shrug. 'My name's Shirley—Shirley Newson. You know my husband, I think?'

Helen said slowly, 'Yes—yes, I do.'

'And wish you didn't, I dare say.' Shirley Newson's smile was affectionate, but wan. 'Trevor's a good man, but when his heart's set on something he turns into a bull in a china shop. I know full well he ruined any chance we had of buying the place. All those stupid ideas about theme parks and the like.' Her eyes flashed. 'As if I'd have allowed that.'

She sighed. 'But I suppose he thought he could make my

dream come true, bless him, and turn a profit at the same time. It's what he's always done, so I can hardly blame him. But all I wanted was to live here quietly, doing the repairs bit by bit. Making it just like it was years ago, when my family worked here. Loving it, I suppose.'

She looked at Helen, biting her lip. 'Now I guess you'll call your security and have me thrown out.'

'Actually,' Helen said gently, 'I was going to offer you a cup of tea, Mrs Newson. And another guided tour—if you'd like that.'

It had been an oddly agreeable couple of hours, Helen decided when her unexpected guest had left. Shirley Newson had spoken no more than the truth when she'd said she knew the house. She was as accurate about its history as Marion Lowell, but she was also a fund of stories—amusing, scandalous and poignant—about the Fraynes and their guests, which her relations had handed down to her, and which Helen, thoroughly intrigued, had never heard before.

Perhaps, she thought wryly, if the wife had come to conduct negotiations a year ago instead of the husband there might have been a different outcome. Perhaps...

Anyway, she thought, it was all too late now. And she sighed.

'You did give Marc my message—about Lottie's wedding?' Helen tried to hide her bitter disappointment as she spoke. 'Because it starts in just over an hour, and he's cutting it incredibly fine if he intends to be here.'

'Mrs Delaroche.' Alan Graham's voice had an edge to it. 'Does it occur to you that there could be—circumstances which might make it difficult for Marc to leave Paris right now?'

Helen bit her lip. 'Meaning Madame Angeline Vallon, I suppose?' she challenged, too hurt and angry to be discreet.

Alan stared at her in open bewilderment. 'You know about that?' he asked incredulously.

'Yes,' she acknowledged curtly. 'After all, it's hardly a secret.'

'You know?' he repeated slowly. 'And yet you carry on with your life as if it didn't matter?' He'd never been friendly, but now he sounded positively hostile.

Riled, Helen lifted her chin. 'Marc makes his own choices,' she said. 'They have nothing to do with me. My world is here.'

His laugh was derisive. 'And so as long as it's looked after you don't give a damn about anything else. I'd hoped that, all appearances to the contrary, you might actually care.'

Care? she thought. *Care?* Can't you see I'm in agony here— falling apart?

She said freezingly, 'You may be my husband's friend, but that gives you no right to criticise me like this.'

'Mrs Delaroche,' he said, 'you are perfectly correct about that, and you can have me removed from this project any time you like. I have other more worthwhile proposals in the pipeline.'

He paused. 'I'm sure Marc will be at this wedding if it's humanly possible. No matter what it may cost him. Because you've asked him to do it. Is that what you want to hear?'

And with a final scornful glance at her, he walked away.

Helen wasn't sure if she had the power to fire him, but she knew she shouldn't let the matter rest. That she should go after him—demand an explanation for his extraordinary behaviour.

Except she had a wedding to dress for, she thought, pushing her hair back from her face with an angry, restless hand. And if she had to attend it alone, she would do so looking like a million dollars.

Because no one was going to accuse her of wearing a broken heart on her sleeve.

She'd decided, after a lot of consideration, to wear her own wedding outfit again. After all, Marc had once suggested that she should do so at a party of their own, she remembered unhappily, and under the circumstances Lottie's wedding reception was probably as good as it was going to get.

But once today was over, she told herself grimly, she would develop some attitude of her own—and deal with Alan Graham.

*   *   *

The service had already begun when she was aware of whispering behind her, and at the same moment Marc slipped into the pew beside her. She turned to look at him, lips parted, delight churning inside her—along with an almost savage yearning.

'I—I didn't think you'd be here,' she breathed.

'I had an invitation.' His whispered reply was cool and unsmiling.

Helen sank back into her seat, her heart thumping painfully. What had she been hoping? That he'd kiss her, murmuring that he could not keep away when all the evidence was to the contrary?

She hadn't been to many traditional weddings, and she'd almost forgotten the timeless resonances of the Prayer Book ceremony. Now they came flooding back with a kind of desperate poignancy, making her hands clench together in her lap and her throat tighten.

She watched Simon and Lottie with painful intensity—his unhidden tenderness, her glorious serenity—knowing that was how it should be when you were safe and loved.

If only Marc had looked at her like that, adoring her with his eyes, when they'd stood together to receive the same blessing the Vicar was pronouncing now, she thought passionately. And if only she'd been free to whisper the oldest vow of all— *I love you* as he bent to kiss her.

Because she knew now with terrible certainty that this was the truth she'd been fighting since she met him. That it wasn't simply the beguilement of sexual union that she'd feared, but the deeper spiritual and emotional commitment that she'd tried to reject. The recognition that in this man—this stranger— she'd somehow met the other half of herself.

Everything else had been a blind—the bargain they'd made, even Monteagle itself.

But only for me, she thought, pain lancing her. Not for Marc. To him it was never more than a deal, and now he has what he wants he's moved on.

She sent him a swift sideways glance from under her lashes,

silently begging him to turn towards her—take her hand. But Marc sat unmoving, his profile like granite, his expression as remote as some frozen wasteland.

And she knew that if there'd been a moment when she might have captured his heart it was long gone. All she was left with was loneliness, stretching out into eternity.

CHAPTER TWELVE

NOT long now, Helen promised herself wearily. The bride and groom had departed for their honeymoon in an aura of radiance, and the usual sense of anticlimax had immediately set in, so the party would soon be breaking up. And just as well, because she was almost at the end of her tether.

She could admit it now. She hadn't felt well all day—tired and vaguely sick. And it had been the same for the past week or more, if she was honest. Stress, she supposed. And sheer uncertainty about the future.

Not that the reception hadn't been a great success. The Long Gallery had looked wonderful, its mellow panelling gleaming in the late sunlight while Lottie's delicious food had been eaten and the toasts drunk, then later assuming an atmosphere of total romance once the candles were lit and the music began.

And Helen couldn't fault Marc. Wherever else he might wish himself to be, he'd behaved like a perfect host. He had danced with practically every woman in the room—bar one. He'd even stood beside her, his hand barely touching her uncovered shoulder, as Simon and Lottie thanked them lavishly for their hospitality and called for their health to be drunk.

'Marc and Helen—who saved our lives.'

And Helen had stood mutely, smiling until her face ached, determined to overcome the churning inside her and trying also to ignore the fact that Marc had not danced with her. Other people had, of course. She'd hardly been a wallflower. But she and her husband had been on parallel lines all evening—never meeting, never touching until that moment. Hardly speaking. And that was clearly the way he wanted it.

Wearing her wedding outfit had been a mistake too. As she'd removed the jacket, her nervous hands struggling once again with those tiny slippery buttons, she'd sensed him near

172

her, and glanced up, wondering if he remembered—if he would come to her rescue this time too. But Marc's dark gaze had swept over her in total indifference, and then he'd turned away, his mouth hardening. And deliberately kept his distance ever after, she realised forlornly.

But when the guests had finally departed and they were left alone—what then?

She'd learned from Daisy that he'd brought a travel bag, which had been put in the State Bedroom. So it seemed he was planning to stay the night at least. But Helen had no idea whether or not he intended to sleep alone, or if, in spite of everything, he would expect her to join him in that vast bed.

The warmth of Lottie's farewell hug and her fierce whisper, 'Be happy', still lingered, taunting her with its sheer impossibility.

Because even if she went to Marc tonight, and he took her, it would mean nothing. Just a transient usage of his marital rights, which she knew she would not have the power to resist. Because she wanted him too badly.

His arms around me, she thought sadly, on any terms. Any terms at all. No pretence. No defence.

And above all she needed to talk to him—to ask him to give their ill-conceived disaster of a marriage another chance. Even if she had to resort to the self-exposure of confessing how much his infidelity was hurting her.

But when she returned from saying goodbye to the bride and groom's parents, and the other departing guests, awash with gratitude and good wishes, the Long Gallery was empty and dark. Daisy and the staff were not scheduled to begin the big clear-up until the morning. But there was no sign of Marc either.

He hadn't even waited to wish her goodnight, let alone offered the chance of the private conversation she needed.

So I'll have to go to him instead, she told herself, taking a deep breath.

The door to the State Bedroom stood slightly ajar, and Helen paused before tapping lightly at its massive panels.

'Entrez.' His voice was brusque, and not particularly welcoming.

When she went in she saw that he'd changed into jeans and a sweatshirt, and was packing the elegant dark suit he'd worn for the wedding into a clothes carrier, his movements swift and economical.

She halted, the breath catching in her throat. 'You're leaving already? You're not staying the night?'

'As you see,' he returned unsmilingly. 'I am expected elsewhere.'

'Where this time?' She tried to speak lightly. 'Kabul? Rio de Janeiro? I can hardly keep pace with your travels.'

'I have to return to Paris.'

'Of course.' Helen lifted her chin. 'Another place that occupies much of your time and attention. But couldn't you delay your trip just a little—please? Go back tomorrow, perhaps, or the next day? I think we need to spend some time together—and talk. Don't you think so?'

'Yes,' he said slowly. 'That will probably be necessary very soon. But not quite yet.' For a long moment he looked at her, the dark eyes scanning her slender body in the pale silk dress, but he took no step towards her.

He added quietly, 'It is essential that I go tonight. Accept my regrets.'

But she was not quite beaten. Not yet. She braced herself for a last throw of the dice.

She said huskily, 'Marc, you—once asked me to go to Paris with you, and I refused. But I could pack very quickly—if you'd consider asking me again.' She stared at him across the space that divided them, her eyes shining with sudden tears. She whispered, 'Please don't leave me again. Take me with you. Keep me with you.' She paused, swallowing. 'Or couldn't you just—forget Paris altogether and stay here?'

She saw a flash of something like pain cross the dark face.

'I am sorry.' His voice was harsh. 'But that is not possible. Please do not ask me to explain.'

But no explanations were necessary, she thought, knifed by desolation. She already knew why there would be no second chance for them. For her. Why he'd decided to shut her out of his life. Angeline Vallon had won, and she was no longer wanted.

Her marriage was over almost before it had begun.

She said quietly, 'I—I'm sorry to have embarrassed you.' And turned to go, praying that she would not break down completely in front of him.

He caught her before she reached the door. 'Hélène.' His voice was low and urgent. 'Ah, *Dieu*. I did not mean it should be like this. Forgive me, if you can.'

Then his mouth was on hers, and he was kissing her with a kind of stark desperation, his lips plundering—bruising—as if he intended to leave his mark on her for ever.

His hands were in the small of her back, pulling her against him, and she was gasping, trembling, her body grinding against his hardness in open longing as desire scalded her. Her arms wound round his neck as her lips parted in trembling, passionate response.

Stay with me...

But he was already detaching himself, putting her away from him. He said hoarsely, 'I cannot do this. I have to go.' There was a kind of agony in his eyes. 'One day, perhaps, you will understand.'

She leaned against the massive frame of the door, listening to the sound of his retreating footsteps.

What was there to understand? she wondered drearily. Only that she'd humbled herself totally to try to win him and been rejected. And now she had to live with the shame of it, she thought. And began to weep very softly.

Helen came out of the doctor's surgery and stood for a moment, as if she wasn't sure which direction to take. She was shivering a little, but whether it was because of the autumnal feeling in the air or the news she'd just received she couldn't be certain.

Why didn't I realise? she asked herself numbly. How could I not have known?

At first she'd attributed her feeling of malaise and the disruption of her monthly routine to the strain imposed by the last

turbulent weeks. But this morning she'd been swiftly and comprehensively sick as soon as she'd got up. And her immediate
shocked suspicion had just been cheerfully confirmed by the
doctor who'd known her all her life.

'Another page in Monteagle's dynasty,' he'd congratulated
her. 'Your husband must be thrilled.'

'I—I haven't mentioned anything to him.' Helen had looked
at her hands, twisted together in her lap. 'Not yet. I wanted to
be sure.'

He'd said once, in a distant past that was somehow only a
few weeks ago, that he wanted children. But since then everything had changed, and she could be certain of nothing.

She had received a keen look. 'I gather this wasn't planned?'

Her lips had formed themselves into a soundless 'no'.

'Then it will be a marvellous surprise for him,' Dr Roscoe
had said confidently, and dismissed her with sensible advice
about the morning sickness and instructions to make another
appointment.

Now, somehow, she found herself outside again, taking great
gulps of air and wondering when exactly this had happened.
She could only hope it had not been during the brief nightmare
of her wedding night, but on that other never-to-be-forgotten
time, when Marc had ravished her body and her senses, un-
aware or uncaring that her heart was already reluctantly his.

But how would he react when he learned she was pregnant?
she asked herself wretchedly. He had not wanted to stay with
her for her own sake. Would he come back for the baby she
was carrying?

Slowly, she turned and began to head back to Monteagle,
her mind treading wearily round the same questions and coming up with uncomfortable answers.

She was so deep in her own thoughts that she hardly realised
where she was, until a familiar voice said, 'You're looking
glum, darling. Trying to figure out where you'll find your next
millionaire?'

Her head came up instantly, defensively, and she met Nigel's
derisive grin. His car was parked on the other side of the road,
outside his parents' empty house with the 'Sold' board in the

garden. And he was here, standing in front of her, the last person she wanted to see.

Strange, she thought, that worrying about Mrs Hartley's good opinion had once been her major problem.

She said, 'What are you doing here?'

He shrugged. 'Mother thought she might have left some things in the roof space, and asked me to check.' He paused. 'I saw you walking past and thought I'd say a last goodbye.'

'Thank you,' she said. 'And—goodbye.'

'I also wanted to say—hard lines.' Nigel detained her, his hand on her arm. 'It looks as if you'll have to sell that expensive heap of yours after all,' he added with a sympathetic whistle.

'I'm sorry,' Helen said coldly, 'but you're not making any sense.'

'No?' He started artistically. 'Then maybe Monsieur Delaroche hasn't told you the bad news. There's been a boardroom revolt in his company—too much going wrong, drop in profits, et cetera—and he's going to be out of a job very soon. Out of money too. He's wasted any fighting fund he might have had pouring money into Monteagle. And there'll be no golden handshake either—not if Hercule Vallon has anything to do with it.'

She said scornfully, 'I don't believe you.'

'Maybe you should take more interest in your husband's affairs,' Nigel drawled. 'His business ones, that is. The board's voting to replace your Marc some time this week, and as his company's his only asset, you're going to need another backer to keep Monteagle. Because he can't afford to.'

He grinned insolently into her shocked face. 'The beautiful Madame Vallon will have her revenge at last. But then you know all about that,' he added insinuatingly. 'You told me so at your wedding.' His smile widened. 'Maybe you should have considered the implications more carefully. You wouldn't have rushed into marriage with such indecent haste if you'd known your millionaire would soon be broke.'

Her heart was hammering and her mouth was dry, but she

managed to say with icy pride, 'I'd have married Marc if he'd been penniless.'

'You married him for Monteagle,' Nigel sneered. 'We all knew that. And once he loses everything do you really think you'll be able to afford to keep the place on? I don't.'

'No,' Helen said quietly. 'Nor do I.' She paused, lifting her chin. 'But I know a woman who will.'

As the taxi took her into the centre of Paris the following day Helen felt strangely relaxed. The calm after the storm this time, she thought.

She had wrung Marc's private address and the whereabouts of his company's head office out of a patently unwilling Alan Graham.

'This is Marc's battle,' he'd kept saying as she had confronted him. 'He didn't want you to know—to be involved.' He gave her a bitter look. 'After all, you only cared about this great white elephant of a house. You never displayed the slightest interest in his work—or his life, for that matter. Why start now?'

'Because I am involved,' she told him. 'I'm his wife, and I'm going to be the mother of his child.' She paused, allowing him to digest that. 'If he's fighting for our lives, then I should be with him.' She paused again. 'Especially as you seem to hold me entirely to blame,' she added drily.

'You came into his life at just the wrong time,' he said bluntly. 'Marc owed his success very much to instinct. He could almost smell political instability—knew when there was trouble brewing. But when he met you he took his eye off the ball. Even when things started to go wrong he thought the company's problems could wait a little while he made sure of you.'

He shrugged. 'But like most successful men he had enemies, and they were soon circling, smelling blood in the water. Given the chance, he could pull things around, and that's what he's been trying to do for the past weeks. But the odds are stacked against him.'

She said, 'And Angeline Vallon? Wasn't she—his mistress? I—I heard—rumours.'

'Angeline Vallon,' Alan said carefully, 'is a self-obsessed bitch, married to a man who's mega-rich and mega-stupid, who lets her do pretty much as she wants. A couple of years back what she wanted most was Marc, but he wasn't interested, and he made the mistake of letting her see it. So she started stalking him—letters—gifts—phone calls. She rented an apartment near his, boasted that they were lovers, tipped off the gossip columns. Turned up at any social event he was attending.

'In the end, he had to take legal action. She was turning his life into a nightmare. And for a while, admittedly, it went quiet. But that was just while she was thinking what to do next. And, of course, she came up with the alternative idea of taking his company away from him. He'd turned her down, so he had to be punished in a way that would hurt him most.

'She made her husband believe—God knows how—that she was the injured party—that Marc had been pursuing her, frightening her with his sexual demands. And, urged on by Angeline, Hercule got together with some of the board who thought they could make a better job of running the company than Marc. All they needed was a window of opportunity.'

He shook his head. 'And when Marc saw you, he left that window wide open.'

She said fiercely, 'Why didn't he tell me any of this?'

His mouth twisted ruefully. 'Because he thought that you only cared about the money—and saving this house. That if he lost the company he'd also lose what little he seemed to have of you.'

His voice deepened harshly. 'We've been friends for years. He always seemed—invincible. Until he met you. You made him vulnerable. And you didn't seem to give a damn about him either.'

He shook his head. 'When I saw him after the honeymoon he was like a stranger—so withdrawn, so wretched. Naturally he wouldn't talk about it, and I couldn't ask. But he no longer seemed to have the will to watch his back, just when he needed to most. And now it's probably too late.'

'No,' Helen said, swiftly and clearly. 'I don't accept that. Oh, why didn't he tell me what was happening?'

Alan was silent for a moment. 'Perhaps because he didn't want you to see him lose?' He hesitated. 'It might be better to wait until he sends for you.'

'But if he loses he may never send for me,' she said. 'And I'm not risking that. Because if he has to start all over again, I intend to be with him.'

It was late afternoon when she reached the Paris offices of Fabrication Roche, only to find the main entrance locked. She rang the bell and a security guard appeared.

She said in her schoolgirl French, 'Where is everyone?'

'They have been sent home, *madame*, following the meeting today.'

Her heart sank like a stone. 'And Monsieur Delaroche?'

'He is still here, *madame*,' the man admitted. 'In the boardroom. But he has given orders not to be disturbed.'

She said briskly, 'I am his wife—Madame Delaroche. Please take me to him at once.'

He gestured helplessly. 'But I have my orders, *madame*, to admit no one.'

Helen stared at him tragically, allowing her lip to tremble convincingly. 'But I have travelled all the way from England, *monsieur*. And I am *enceinte*. These rules cannot apply to me.'

She could never be sure whether it was her announcement that she was pregnant or the threat of tears that did it, but next minute she was in a high-powered lift, travelling to the top floor.

At the end of the short passage a pair of double doors confronted her. She opened them and slipped inside.

Marc was standing by the huge picture window at the end of the room, silhouetted against the fading afternoon light. His bent head and his arms folded tautly across his body spoke of a weariness and tension almost too great to be borne. And of a loneliness that tore at her heart.

She put down her travel bag. 'Marc,' she said softly. 'Marc, darling.'

He turned abruptly, his eyes narrowing in disbelief. 'Hélène—what are you doing here?'

She walked towards him. 'I made myself homeless this morning,' she said. 'I was hoping you might offer me a bed for the night. Or for quite a lot of nights. The rest of our lives, even.'

His mouth tightened. He said, 'Is this some game?'

'No,' she said. 'I'm deadly serious. You see—I've sold Monteagle.'

'Sold it?' His hands gripped her arms. He stared down into her face. 'But that is not possible. It is your home, the centre of your life.'

She said steadily, 'Marc, you're the centre of my life. Nothing else matters. So Monteagle now belongs to Trevor Newson—every brick, every beam, every blade of grass. All except the portrait of Helen Frayne,' she added. 'And Alan's taking care of that for us.'

He let her go, stepping backwards, his face a mask of consternation. 'You sold to Trevor Newson—to that man? But you loathe him—and his plans for Monteagle. You have always said so.'

'Yes,' she agreed. 'But I don't think his schemes will be as bad as I thought. He's buying the house primarily for his wife, and I suspect she won't let him go too far. Besides,' she added, shrugging, 'I won't be there to see what happens. I'll be with you, if you want me. And if you don't hate me too much for selling the place you loved so much.'

'I loved it for your sake, Hélène,' he said quietly. 'Because I adored you, *mon amour*, and I wanted only to make you happy.'

'And now perhaps I can make it up to you in turn, for losing Fabrications Roche.' She took an envelope from her jacket pocket. 'Marc, darling, this is for you. It's in your name.'

'*Comment?*' He was frowning as he tore open the envelope, then he stopped, his lips parting in a gasp of sheer astonishment as he saw the amount on the bank draft it contained. '*Mon Dieu!* He paid you this much?'

'Without a murmur,' she said. 'Egged on by the wonderful

Shirley. Alan and the bank manager advised me what to ask, and I think I could have got more.' She paused. 'But it's enough, isn't it?' she asked almost diffidently. 'Enough for us to start again—together? Begin a life—a real marriage? Because I love you, and I don't think I can live without you.'

He stared at her in silence and she tried to laugh, the memory of his last rejection burning in her. 'Marc—please. Haven't you got anything to say?'

He said unsteadily, 'I think I am afraid to speak in case I awake and find that I have been dreaming.'

Helen moved to him, sliding her arms round his waist under his jacket, pressing herself close to him. She whispered, 'Do I feel like a dream?' His body quickened and hardened against hers. 'Because you feel incredibly real.'

'*Ah, mon ange.*' He sank down to the floor, pulling her with him to the thick carpet. Their hands tugged and tore at each other's clothing, made clumsy by haste and need. She returned his kisses eagerly, moaning faintly as his hands uncovered and caressed her naked breasts, then lifted herself towards him, sobbing with acceptance as he entered her.

He said thickly, '*Hélène—je t'aime—je t'adore.*'

'Yes,' she whispered, her voice shaking as she began to move with him, their bodies blending hungrily. 'Oh, my love—my love…'

It was not a prolonged mating. Their mutual desire was too fierce, too greedy for its satisfaction. As the soft, trembling pulsations deep within her reached their culmination she cried out, and heard him groan his pleasure in turn.

When she could speak again, Helen said faintly, 'Thank heaven I packed some stuff. You've wrecked this dress completely.'

'I hope you do not want me to apologise.' He wrapped her closely in his arms, his lips against her hair. 'Perhaps you should stop wearing clothes altogether.'

'With winter coming?' Helen pretended to shiver. 'Besides,' she added, trying to sound casual, 'the baby might catch a chill.'

His caressing hand abruptly stopped its ministrations. 'Baby? What are you saying?'

'Yes, darling,' she told him softly. 'That's the other thing I came to tell you. It seems you're going to be a father.'

'*Ah, Dieu.*' He lifted himself on to an elbow, staring at her in a kind of anguish. 'What have I done?'

She looked back at him, her throat tightening in shock. 'You—don't want our baby? I admit the timing isn't ideal, but—'

'Want it?' He seized her hands, covering them in kisses. '*Mon coeur*, I cannot believe such happiness. But we should not have made love,' he added grimly. 'It could be dangerous when you are only just *enceinte.*'

'Well, the baby will just have to cope.' She smiled up at him. 'We have to make up for lost time, my love.'

'Then I shall have to learn to be gentle. You have to be kept safe, even if I have to wrap you in silk,' Marc told her softly.

'Safe.' She sighed the word. 'The first time you made me feel safe was when I'd had too much to drink and you slept with me on the sofa.' Her eyes widened. 'I think that was when I realised I was falling in love with you.'

He framed her face between his hands. 'And yet you ran away,' he reminded her teasingly. 'Why didn't you awaken me, Hélène, and tell me how you felt—what you wanted me to do?' he added, kissing her mouth softly and sensuously.

'Because Nigel had told me you exercised a two-month limit on your affairs, and I was frightened,' she said frankly. 'Scared to love you, or let you make love to me, in case you broke my heart.'

'But with you, it was never to be an *affaire*,' he said quietly. 'It was to be a lifetime. Because you were the one I had been waiting for, *cherie*. The girl of my heart. With the others before you—' he shrugged '—I can say only in my defence that I tried to be honest—to make no promises I would not keep, nor offer commitment I would not fulfil. When they knew there was no future in the relationship, most of my girlfriends walked away.'

She said in a low voice, 'But with me, you always said it was the house you wanted. And I was just part of the deal.'

'I said that to protect myself. And to stop you running away from me. You see, *mon amour*, at that time I thought you still cared for Nigel.'

'Nigel!' Helen sat up indignantly. 'Oh, you couldn't have done.'

'I saw you together at the wedding,' he said, his mouth twisting. 'You seemed quite happy in his arms.'

She said flatly, 'I think I was temporarily paralysed. He was telling me to ask you about Angeline Vallon. He—he implied she was your mistress.'

'And you believed him?' His voice was incredulous. 'But why did you not ask me?'

'Because I couldn't guarantee what your answer might be,' she said. She took a deep breath. 'I'm afraid I'd heard you talking to Alan about her, and I'm not proud of that. Nigel appeared to confirm what you'd said. So heartbreak seemed to be right there, waiting for me.' She paused. 'Anyway, why didn't you ask me about Nigel?'

'Because I told myself that once we were married, and in bed together, I could make you forget him,' he said huskily. 'That I could persuade you to fall in love with me. I was that arrogant—that stupid. I should have known that with you it could never be that simple.'

'I fought you for my own sake,' she said quietly. 'No one else's. But I still could not stop myself wanting you.' She was silent for a moment. 'That money—I gave it to the poor in St Benoit.'

His smile was crooked as he drew her back into his arms and lay down again, her head pillowed on his chest. 'How estimable of you, *cherie*.'

'I wish I hadn't now,' she said regretfully. 'After all, we need every penny we can get.'

He laughed. 'Things are not that bad, *ma petite*.'

'Marc—don't pretend. Alan told me you stood to lose everything.' She stirred uneasily. 'I don't suppose we should even be here—especially, my goodness, like this,' she added, recognising their joint state of *dishabille*. 'The security men might come to escort you from the building. Isn't that what happens? And don't you have a desk to clear? Because I could help…'

'Hélène,' he said gently. 'Do not upset yourself. There is no need, I promise.'

'I'm bound to be upset,' she protested. 'You've lost Fabrication Roche, and I know what it meant to you. How difficult it must be…'

'*Mon coeur,*' he said patiently, 'I did not lose. It was close, but I won. I still have the company.'

She stared up at him, open-mouthed. 'But Alan said—'

'Alan is a realist. He knew the odds were against me. But I had suspected a long time ago that someone might be planning a boardroom *coup*. We were suddenly encountering problems where there had been none before.' Wryly, he counted them on his fingers. 'Sabotage, strikes, accusations of racism, key workers abducted and held to ransom.'

He shook his head. 'Someone wished to acquire Fabrication Roche, and cheaply, but I did not at once see that Angeline Vallon might be involved. I thought that difficulty was behind me—that she had seen the error of her ways. But I was wrong.

'However, I knew that I had not been her only target. Not all of them had resisted, *naturellement*, but they had all found it was not easy to escape her talons, even when the relationship had palled and they wished it to end. She had a capacity for revenge, that one.'

Helen's eyes were like saucers. 'But her husband…'

'He worshipped her,' Marc said briefly. 'And she dominated him. He decided that her beauty made her the prey of other men's lusts, but that she was always innocent. I had insulted her, therefore I must be punished. He has a simplistic mind, *le pauvre* Hercule.'

His mouth twisted. 'And, as Alan saw, I had allowed my attention to wander a little. But what could I do, once I had seen the woman I had been waiting for all my life? I had to make you mine.'

She nestled closer. 'You were certainly persistent.'

He kissed her again. 'I was in love. So much so that I could almost understand poor foolish Hercule. That day when I sat beside you at Charlotte's wedding I knew I would give anything to have you look at me as she did at her husband, but it seemed hopeless. And I was afraid, too, that if I could not afford Monteagle I might lose you for ever.'

'But I came to you,' she said. 'I offered myself. You know that.'

'I did not know, however, what I could offer in return.' He stroked the curve of her cheek. 'I was scared that if it was a choice between Monteagle and myself, I would lose. So it seemed best to fight on alone, until I knew what kind of life I could lay at your feet.'

'And I thought you preferred Angeline Vallon and couldn't wait to get back to her,' she confessed.

'In a way, you were right. My legal advisers had contacted me to say that they had finally drawn up a dossier of her affairs, with testimony from her other victims. So I was able to present it to Hercule before the final meeting today and watch him collapse. It was not pleasant, and I felt,' he added quietly, 'like a murderer.

'But his bid for Fabrication Roche collapsed with him, along with his allies on the board.' His smile was grim. 'They were the ones who found themselves being escorted from the building. Now there will be some restructuring and—*voilà*—life goes on.'

'So you didn't actually need the money I brought you.' There was a touch of wistfulness in her voice.

'Ah, but I needed the love that came with it.' His arms tightened round her. 'And the look in your eyes I had prayed for. A far more precious gift, *mon amour*.' He paused, his hand caressing the curve of her body that sheltered his child.

'Although,' he added. 'We could use the money, if you wish, to try and repurchase Monteagle.'

She shook her head slowly. 'No, that's all in the past, and I'd rather let it go—invest in our future. Find a new home for us both, and our children.' She hesitated. 'Marc—when I came in, you didn't look like someone who'd just won a famous victory. You looked—sad.'

'I was thinking of you,' he said quietly. 'And all the mistakes I had made. Wondering how soon I could go to you—to explain and ask you to forgive me. To try once more to persuade you to let me share your life—to love me. It seemed at that moment my real battle was still to come. Until you spoke, and smiled at me, and I realised that, little as I deserved it, I had been offered a miracle.'

He bent and took her mouth, gently and reverently.

'And now,' he told her, 'I must get you dressed and fed, my wife. But the only bed I can offer is in my apartment,' he added ruefully. 'And you have never wished to go there.'

'I thought I had my reasons,' she said. 'But I was wrong. About so many things.' She allowed him to lift her to her feet, and slid her arms round his neck, her eyes shining into his with joy and trust. 'Please, Marc—take me home.'

eHARLEQUIN.com

The Ultimate Destination for Women's Fiction

The eHarlequin.com online community is *the* place to share opinions, thoughts and feelings!

- Joining the community is easy, fun and **FREE!**

- Connect with **other romance fans** on our message boards.

- Meet your **favorite authors** without leaving home!

- **Share opinions** on books, movies, celebrities…and *more!*

Here's what our members say:

"I love the friendly and helpful atmosphere filled with support and humor."
—Texanna (eHarlequin.com member)

"Is this the place for me, or what? There is nothing I love more than 'talking' books, especially with fellow readers who are reading the same ones I am."
—Jo Ann (eHarlequin.com member)

Join today by visiting
www.eHarlequin.com!

HARLEQUIN®
Presents~

The world's bestselling romance series...
The series that brings you your favorite authors,
month after month:

Helen Bianchin...Emma Darcy
Lynne Graham...Penny Jordan
Miranda Lee...Sandra Marton
Anne Mather...Carole Mortimer
Susan Napier...Michelle Reid

and many more uniquely talented authors!

Wealthy, powerful, gorgeous men...
Women who have feelings just like your own...
The stories you love, set in exotic, glamorous locations...

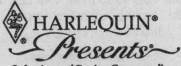